"It's not often o   opportunity to mix business with pleasure the way we could, Chattie," he added musingly.

That did it. The explosion he was waiting for—had even hoped to provoke?—came. She sprang up with her fists clenched and opened her mouth.

"Let me guess," he murmured, and got up himself. "I'd be the last man on the planet you'd marry? You'd rather socialize with a snake?"

Chattie closed her mouth, almost biting her tongue as he took the words right out of it.

"Don't you think you are kidding yourself?" he added softly, but lethally, as he came to stand right in front of her.

She took a distraught breath. "No."

"Well, I do." He reached for her. "This morning you told me it was rather lovely to be in my arms. What can have changed?"

"You've changed," she said bitterly.

THE AUSTRALIANS

Where spirited women win the hearts of
Australia's most eligible men!

Experience the romance of Australia,
as only the bestselling authors from
Harlequin Presents® can imagine.

Coming soon to a store near you.

Lindsay Armstrong

THE AUSTRALIAN'S CONVENIENT BRIDE

THE AUSTRALIANS

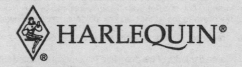

HARLEQUIN®

TORONTO • NEW YORK • LONDON
AMSTERDAM • PARIS • SYDNEY • HAMBURG
STOCKHOLM • ATHENS • TOKYO • MILAN • MADRID
PRAGUE • WARSAW • BUDAPEST • AUCKLAND

ISBN 0-373-12426-0

THE AUSTRALIAN'S CONVENIENT BRIDE

First North American Publication 2004.

Copyright © 2004 by Lindsay Armstrong.

CHAPTER ONE

STEVE KINANE turned off the highway, swore beneath his breath and pulled his Range Rover off the dirt road towards the girl thumbing a lift on this isolated outback road.

Country ethics dictated that you didn't ignore any travellers in distress but it had been a long day and he got the feeling he was about to be taken out of his way. Then he noticed—and this slightly qualified his 'damsel in distress' reading of the situation—that she had an efficient and fit-looking bodyguard: a blue heeler with black points on a lead. While only medium-sized dogs, their devotion to duty was legendary.

He opened his door cautiously and the dog barked but, at one word from its mistress, sank silently to its haunches, Steve firmly in its sights.

'Hello,' he said, approaching the girl. 'Where are you headed?'

She was a cool, young blonde—in her early twenties, he guessed. Her hair was long, fair, curly, and tied back under a blue linen sunhat. Her eyes were grey and direct and her figure in jeans and a T-shirt—his eyes widened—was slim and curvy.

'Afternoon,' she replied. 'Thanks for stopping. I'm headed for Mount Helena station. I think it's about ten miles down the road.'

He frowned. 'Are they expecting you?'

'Does that mean you know it?' she countered politely, taking in his stained, frayed jeans, his bush shirt, battered boots and dirty hands.

He looked down at himself and said, not entirely truthfully, 'I—work there.' Then immediately wondered why he was being selective with the truth—obviously some instinct he couldn't pinpoint was directing him.

But the girl seemed to relax. 'I'd really appreciate a lift, then. This isn't the busiest of roads, is it?' She looked nervously at the empty landscape before turning to look straight back at him. 'I'm Charlotte Winslow, by the way,' she said without dropping her gaze and while confidently putting out her hand.

He took it, noticing that her arm was lightly tanned with skin as smooth as silk. The dog growled warningly.

'It's OK, Rich,' she murmured, but instantly withdrew her hand.

'I'm sorry, but Charlotte Winslow doesn't ring a bell,' he said.

'Please call me Chattie, everyone does,' she invited. 'Uh—they may not have had time to discuss me with—uh—you.'

'They may not have,' he replied sardonically and allowed his cool, dark gaze to drift down her figure again.

She took a sharp breath as she suffered the paralysing experience of being mentally undressed before his eyes narrowed and focused on hers again. 'Are you after Mark Kinane, by any chance?'

She hesitated. 'What makes you think that?'

'It's been known,' he replied. 'Are you?'

Chattie debated for a moment, and decided the simplest way to go would be to admit to it and let this man make whatever he liked of it. 'Yes.'

'How come?'

She chewed her lip. 'We, that is, Mark, talked a bit about the place and he issued an open invitation, so here I am!' Surely he can tell I'm lying, she thought.

'How the hell did you get this far?' Steve Kinane asked incredulously.

'I got a lift from Brisbane with a friend who was going through to Augathella. He would have brought me the whole way but it wasn't a four-wheel-drive and he didn't want to risk his suspension off the highway on this kind of road.'

She looked expressively westward along the dusty red road with its potholes, gutters and ridges.

'What would you have done if no one had come along?'

She shrugged, hopefully disguising her own surprise that her friend had just abandoned her here. 'I was going to give it another hour, then walk back to the highway. I'd have had no trouble getting a lift to the nearest town and—tomorrow is another day.'

'OK,' he said at last. 'The dog can go in the back with your bag.' He heaved up her holdall.

Five minutes later they were all aboard and under way with the dog planted alertly in the back seat. To his irritation, Steve could feel it breathing down the back of his neck.

Chattie, on the other hand, couldn't help but be impressed by his expert handling of the vehicle on such a difficult road and it came to her unwittingly that this employee of Mount Helena station, with his strong hands and long lines, was rather a fine figure of a man. She even felt herself blush as these thoughts brought back the memory of his visual exploration of her body earlier.

Stunned by the direction of her thoughts, she immediately and sternly told herself she must be out of her mind, this was not the time or place for anything of that nature, and she concentrated fiercely on the countryside instead. Still vast, it wasn't quite so empty now, she noticed, with some interesting rocky outcrops and more trees.

Then her lift said, 'How long have you known Mark, Chattie Winslow?'

She thought back carefully. 'A few months, I guess.'

He flicked her a glance. She'd taken off her hat and her profile was delicious. A short, straight little nose, lovely curving mouth, delicately sculptured jaw and a smooth, slender throat. Even her ear, and it occurred to him he'd never really considered ears before, was pretty with that riotous fair hair tucked behind it.

I have to hand it to you, Mark, he thought, you sure can pick 'em, although why do I get the feeling you may have bitten off more than you can chew here?

'How did you meet Mark?' he asked.

'At a party,' Chattie answered honestly but conscious at the same time that, in her quest to keep things simple, she was presenting herself in the light of Mark Kinane's girlfriend, which could complicate things for her. She added, with a smile curving her lips to take the sting out of it, 'Why do I get the feeling you're interrogating me?'

A corner of his mouth twitched; it had been an enchanting smile. 'Just interested. I guess you're a bit of a diversion from damn cows.' He waved a hand at a mob of cattle gathered around a small dam. 'Sometimes they're enough to send you stir-crazy.'

Chattie looked ahead and laughed, an attractive musical sound. 'I guess I can understand that. I believe Mark felt the same.' She stopped and bit her lip. Until she found Mark Kinane, she didn't want to discuss him with anyone, let alone an employee, so why did she keep bringing up his name?

'I could tell you something about me,' she offered. 'I'm a teacher.'

The Range Rover veered off course briefly until he corrected it.

'What's so surprising about that?' she asked, amused at his reaction.

'You don't look like a teacher.' He flicked her another glance, but this time she met it and their gazes caught and held for a brief, but telling, moment.

Trying not to sound as shaken as she felt, she said, 'Thanks, but your ideas about teachers could be a bit outdated.'

'Perhaps.' He shrugged. 'What do you teach?'

'Domestic Science—as in cooking and sewing, which is rather lucky because I love to do both.'

Curiouser and curiouser, Steve Kinane reflected. His brother Mark's taste in women didn't run along domestic lines, or hadn't to date. Models and starlets had featured prominently in his love life: beautiful, flighty creatures with few practical talents that he'd been able to detect, at least.

Yet, although this girl had the looks, she not only taught down-to-earth, practical subjects, but, if the way she'd got herself this far into the outback and the way she'd trained her dog was anything to go by, she was both practical and down-to-earth herself.

'Is there anything wrong with that?' Chattie enquired as the silence stretched.

'Not at all,' he denied, but added the silent rider to himself—Just doesn't make sense.

'I also paint and play the piano,' she offered gravely, but now he got the distinct impression she was laughing at him.

'What do you know about Mount Helena?' he asked abruptly.

Chattie searched through her knowledge of the place and found it to be minimal. 'Er—not a lot.'

He glanced at her suspiciously. 'Mark must have told you something!'

Chattie detected both the suspicion and the fact that he was less than amused. On the heels of this discovery came the realization that he might only be an employee but he was also tall and tough and quite capable of questioning her right to be ferried to Mount Helena. And equally capable of turning back and dumping her on the highway if he decided she was less than legitimate.

'Uh—I gather that Mark hasn't decided whether he wants to be a cattleman yet but he did say it was quite a place. I've never seen a cattle station.'

'Go on.'

It was definitely an order and Chattie bristled. 'What more do you want to know? He has an older brother who runs the place and goes around like a dictator, but if you work there you probably know that as well as anyone.'

Whether prompted by her tone or his, Rich growled softly as if to back her up.

Steve Kinane looked irritated beyond words but the glint of suspicion died out of his eyes, although he did say, 'You obviously have no qualms about foisting your dog on unsuspecting hosts?'

'He's trained to sleep outside, if necessary, and I'd be more than happy to introduce him to anyone he needs to know so they needn't be scared of him. He's actually a very friendly dog,' she said evenly.

'So long as no one raises a hand or their voice to you.'

Their gazes clashed briefly.

'When I found Rich he'd been abandoned as a puppy in a box in a building rubble dumpster,' she said coolly. 'How he wasn't crushed I'll never know. I had to climb into the bin and literally dig him out. He's been my constant companion ever since.'

'As well as suitably grateful and devoted,' Steve commented, but as her eyes flashed added, 'Don't get your hackles up, I would have done the same.'

He turned the wheel and drove through a set of wire gates and they trundled over a cattle-grid. The legend on the gates—MOUNT HELENA—was not flashy but the road improved immediately.

'Nearly there, I gather?' Chattie hazarded.

'Yep, about a mile to go.'

They drove the last mile in silence until Steve pulled up outside a garden fence.

Chattie looked through the windscreen at the sprawling white-painted house with a red tin roof beyond the fence. It was surrounded by lawn and shrubbery and neatly fenced off, everything was neat and trim for that matter and although the house was old, it gleamed with new paint. Behind it were several water tanks smothered with bougainvillea and allamanda, and the land rose from there to a series of low hills cloaked in gold grass studded with blackboys.

Marvellous colours, she thought, taking in the red-gold soil, the sky, the grass and the house again, and she heaved a sudden sigh of relief.

Steve Kinane glinted a question at her.

She smiled with a touch of embarrassment. 'It looks quite civilized.'

'You expected to have to rough it?'

'I wasn't quite sure, to be honest. Mark, well, most men,' she amended hastily, 'aren't very good at describing houses, are they?'

Steve didn't reply but had she thought to check his expression, Chattie would have discovered it to be rather grimly thoughtful.

Then he shrugged and opened his door. 'I'll drop you off here. The—uh—housekeeper should be around somewhere—oh, there he is. I'll just have a word with him.'

Chattie blinked. The 'housekeeper' was a tough, leathery-looking man in his forties with a bald pate and grey pony-tail. Steve met him at the garden gate but their conversation was inaudible, although Chattie did observe that there seemed to be an aura of incredulity about it. There was certainly a bit of head-shaking on the part of the housekeeper.

Then her lift—it was at this point that Chattie realized she didn't know his name—brought the other man over to introduce him.

'Chattie, this is Slim,' he said through the window.

'He's in charge of the house and he'll look after you until…things get sorted out.'

'How do you do, Slim?' She stuck her hand out of the window to have it taken in a strong grip. Rich barked.

'Howdy,' Slim said in a deep, gravelly voice as he ducked his head to look in at her. 'Well, I'll be…' He didn't finish as his gaze ran over Chattie and the dog. 'That is to say, welcome to Helena, miss.'

'Thank you,' Chattie replied. 'Is Mark around?'

'Not at present,' Slim replied.

'Oh.' She looked uncertain.

'Doesn't mean to say we can't make you comfortable,' Slim offered. 'Let's get your gear out. Is the dog house-trained?'

Chattie explained that it certainly was and received the information that the house was between dogs at the moment but there would be no objection to a suitably trained one taking up temporary residence.

She couldn't help herself from raising her eyebrows at the man who had driven her here, only to be ignored, and not much later she was installed in a guest suite beneath the red roof of the Mount Helena homestead.

Slim had provided her with afternoon tea on a tray. He'd also advised her that dinner was scheduled for seven o'clock and recommended that she not bother about unpacking but have a rest instead.

Her lift had disappeared before she could thank him or discover his name.

Her question to Slim about when she could expect to see Mark Kinane had been answered with a shrug and a negligent wave of his hand—as if to say she shouldn't bother her head about it. Then she'd been left alone.

She sat down on the vast bed and Rich sat at her feet with his head on her knee. 'Why—' she stroked his nose and spoke with a frown '—am I getting strange vibes? Don't tell me I've come on a wild-goose chase and Mark isn't here?'

She looked around. Although rather old-fashioned, it was a large, comfortable room with a covered, screened veranda and its own bathroom.

In fact, everything in the bedroom was on a grand scale. Big bed, large mahogany wardrobe with an oval mirror in the central panel, divine chest of drawers starting small at the top, the drawers, and graduating to full width towards the floor. Pretty curtains in an old-fashioned floral cretonne with twisted cord tie-backs and a rose-red sumptuous silk-covered eider-down on the bed.

The bathroom appeared to have been modernized recently, the veranda had two comfortable cane chairs and a table on it and the whole was spotlessly clean and polished.

But as she poured then sipped her tea gratefully her thoughts turned to the predicament, or one of them anyway, she appeared to have got herself into—suspected of being Mark Kinane's girlfriend, in other words. Of course, she acknowledged, the whole reason for her being at Mount Helena had all the hallmarks of a tragic predicament, but for her sister Bridget.

Mind you, she sighed, since she and her younger sister had been orphaned and placed in the care of an aunt who had found them burdensome, Bridget had been a predicament in her own right. Even now, at nineteen, absolutely lovely and training to be a model, she was as vulnerable and defenceless as she had been from the time of the loss of their parents.

Or, Chattie suddenly wondered, was she always destined to be the same? Warm, loving, generous, scatty and staggeringly unwise at times without me to lend a guiding hand?

And was I always destined to feel responsible for her, to sometimes feel a hundred years older than her although I'm only twenty-two?

She sighed again and put her cup back on the tray. Whatever, when Mark Kinane had entered their lives at a party and completely bewitched Bridget with his good looks and fun ways, she had done her level best to keep Bridget's feet on the ground. Her utmost to prevent her sister from being swept *off* her feet and then her warmest and wisest when Mark and Bridget had broken up and she'd been left to pick up the pieces.

The only time she'd lost her cool had been when Bridget had shown her a positive home-pregnancy-test kit and announced that it was Mark's baby and she would never love anyone else.

'Does he know?' she'd cried with utter frustration. And—'How did it happen?'

He didn't know because Bridget had not known herself at the time. How it had happened had been typical Bridget, a tale of mixed-up dates and forgotten pills, or perhaps the one night they'd both got so carried away it hadn't entered their minds?

For the first time in her life, Chattie had been really stern with her sister and she'd dragged the whole story of the breakup out of her rather than the edited version she'd suspected she'd been favoured with to date.

Mark Kinane, who was the same age as Chattie, was a mixed-up young man, it emerged. He'd already suffered a broken engagement, he wasn't sure what course his life should take and he'd been ordered home to an outback cattle station by his disapproving older brother.

As it transpired, Bridget laid a lot of the blame for Mark's difficulties and insecurities at the dictatorial older brother's feet—he'd been their father's favourite, according to Bridget.

He was forcing Mark to be something he didn't want to be, he was perpetually undermining his confidence, but with she, Bridget, at his side, her sister had declared passionately, along with the responsibility of a family, things would be very different.

Chattie had reviewed Mark Kinane in her mind's eye and not been so sure at all. Charming he'd been, yes. Hard to resist, yes, but how much substance there was to him and whether this news would be welcome were another matter. One thing she couldn't dispute, however, was that he had a right to know and Bridget's baby had a right to some kind of support.

It had been when Bridget had decided categorically that she could only deliver this news to Mark in person that Chattie had decided otherwise. Bridget was looking fragile, haunted and starting to suffer from morning sickness—there was no way she could go chasing what might turn out to be moonbeams beyond the black stump. Chattie would go herself.

The outpouring of love and gratitude from Bridget had been moving but Chattie had taken two precautions. She'd rung the station and asked for Mark Kinane only to be told he was out on a muster and would she like to leave a message? She'd declined, saying she would call back, which she'd had no intention of doing but at least she'd established where he was—she guessed now it was Slim she'd spoken to. And she'd installed a good friend in their rented cottage to keep an eye on Bridget while she was away, just in case things took time...

'Perhaps I had a premonition? Or, perhaps I'm imagining things. If he was here two days ago, surely he's still here?' she said to Rich, now curled up at her feet.

He opened an eye and thumped his tail.

She smiled. 'None of the aforementioned answers the question of what to do about being mistaken for Mark's girlfriend, though.'

This time the dog scratched his ear and she laughed softly. 'I know, it's a right old conundrum! Oh, well, maybe I'll just play it by ear. If the guy who picked us up is anything to go by, they're a pretty cagey lot.'

This conjured up a mental vision of their 'lift' and she frowned. Was it her imagination or had there been something...she couldn't find the right words...but something more to him than a worker on a cattle station not precisely beyond the black stump but certainly in remote western Queensland?

She pictured him again in her mind's eye, searching for that elusive quality, but could only come up with: dusty and dirty he might have been, but rather dishy with thick dark hair, dark eyes and a fine physique.

'Probably got from throwing a lot of calves,' she told herself dismissively, only to find that he wasn't so easy to dismiss from her thoughts. In fact it was difficult to think of him at all without thinking of his hands, his tall strength and the curious fact that being undressed mentally by him had annoyed her, yes, but hadn't entirely left her cold…

Stop it, she advised herself, then yawned with genuine weariness. It had been a big day, mentally and physically.

She'd had no intention of taking Slim's advice about delaying her unpacking and having a rest but the desire to lie down and close her eyes just for a few minutes was irresistible.

Two hours later she woke with a jerk. It was dark and for a moment she was completely disorientated, then she remembered and grimaced.

She groped for the bedside lamp and, by its soft glow, discovered it was six-thirty. She listened for a moment but heard no sounds.

'OK, boy, enough of this sloth,' she commanded as she got up.

Rich bounded up and together they descended to the lawn below the veranda. Slim had told Chattie that the station dogs were barred from the garden, but all the same, Chattie put a lead on the dog while they stretched their legs.

'Not much exercise but it will have to do,' Chattie murmured as they got back to the bedroom and went to take a shower.

She was just ready when someone knocked on her door. It was Slim.

'Dinner's nearly ready, miss, and Mr Kinane has asked you to join him for a drink.'

'Mark?'

Slim shook his head. 'By the way, I've made up a meal for your dog—think he'd come with me?'

Chattie thanked him warmly and was just about to hand over Rich when she was struck by a thought. 'How many Mr Kinanes are there? I mean, as far as I know, Mark has no father and only one brother.'

'That's him. I'll show you the way,' Slim offered.

Chattie swallowed, then tilted her chin. 'Thank you.'

Steve Kinane paused in the act of raising a glass of Scotch to his mouth as he heard Slim say, 'In here, miss.'

He turned to the lounge doorway—and encountered a pair of stunned grey eyes.

Charlotte Winslow had changed for dinner. So had he, for that matter, but only into clean jeans and a fresh, well-pressed khaki shirt, whereas she looked sensational.

Her hair was loose, in a curly bob to just above her shoulders, and very fair beneath the overhead light. Her outfit was simple yet elegant: cream trousers and a toffee-coloured silky blouse but, simple though it was, it showed off her lovely figure to perfection.

She was also, he realized, the only person he'd ever met who could look attractive with their mouth hanging open in disbelief.

He grimaced. 'Come in, Chattie. What would you like to drink?'

She shut her mouth then said through her teeth, 'Are you who I think you are?'

'I'm Steve Kinane, Mark's older brother—the dictator, no less.'

CHAPTER TWO

'WHY didn't you *tell* me?'

Steve shrugged. 'I wondered if there was something you weren't telling me, to be honest, Miss Winslow. *Would* you like a drink?'

Chattie considered him out of smouldering eyes. 'I could certainly do with one.'

He raised an eyebrow at her. 'Name your poison.'

'If you had anything resembling a glass of chilled white wine—'

'Done.' He put his glass down and opened a cabinet to reveal a bar fridge.

Chattie watched as he opened a bottle of wine.

Steve Kinane bore little resemblance to his brother Mark. He would be in his early thirties, but whereas Mark was fair and elegant with blue eyes, this man, with his dark hair and eyes, reminded her of a sturdy tree. He was as tall as Mark, over six feet, and, as she'd noted earlier, he was extremely fit-looking, but—how come she'd failed to pin down that elusive something about him as a definite air of command befitting the owner of Mount Helena?

None of it impressed her particularly at that moment, however, and her expression obviously gave this away as he handed her a glass of wine.

'Sit down and relax,' he invited with a dry little smile twisting his lips.

She glanced around and chose an armchair covered

in green velour. The lounge of Mount Helena home-stead was furnished along the same grand lines as the guest bedroom—lots of mahogany and cedar but a rather attractive colour scheme of sage green and to-paz.

He took his drink over to a matching armchair and sat down opposite. 'So?'

Chattie fortified herself with a sip of wine. 'I'm try-ing to guess what you imagine I'm *not* telling you,' she said coolly at last.

He observed that the finely sculptured chin he'd been admiring earlier was tilted to an ominous angle, and turned his glass in his hands. 'Why you're running after my brother—how about that for starters?' he suggested.

'What makes you think I'm running after him?'

'The manner of your—completely unexpected—arrival,' he answered thoughtfully. 'The fact that it *has* happened before and, I may as well tell you this right away, the fact that I plan to send you back where you came from just as soon as I can.'

She gasped. *'Why?'*

'Because Mark left Mount Helena two days ago.'

Chattie stared at him, and repeated herself. 'Why?'

Steve Kinane took a pull of his Scotch and watched her narrowly. 'When did you last hear from him?'

She blinked a couple of times. 'What does that have to do with it? Incidentally, what has any of this got to do with *you*? And if you knew Mark wasn't here why didn't you tell me immediately?'

He sat back. 'I didn't know. I've been out working on a bore for a couple of days. I only discovered his—er—defection this afternoon.'

Chattie licked her lips as she thought of Bridget sitting in Brisbane wringing her hands. 'Where has he gone?' she asked huskily. 'And why would he have gone so suddenly?'

'This is only an educated guess but his ex-fiancée—' he paused as he scanned Chattie thoroughly for any reaction but she only looked blank '—lives in Broome. He may be having second thoughts about her. As for why he went so suddenly, Mark and Mount Helena—' Steve Kinane looked satanically irritated '—only go together in small doses.'

Chattie couldn't restrain herself from making a strangled little sound of mixed emotions—frustration, confusion and a growing feeling of desperation.

'Did he neglect to tell you about her?' Steve enquired, his eyes dark and cool. 'I would imagine he broke off the engagement just before he met you.'

'I...that's...that is to say...' Chattie drained her wine and shuddered visibly.

'You would not be the only girl who thought herself madly in love with my brother only to find he had feet of clay,' Steve Kinane said dryly. 'Or the only girl to chase him round the countryside.'

'Dinner's ready,' Slim announced from the archway that led into the dining room.

'I don't feel hungry, thank you,' Chattie said automatically.

Slim came into the lounge with his hands on his hips. 'Not hungry? When I've spent all afternoon slaving over a hot stove to concoct a nice dinner?'

'Miss Winslow has had a bit of a shock,' Steve murmured.

'Lovie,' Slim addressed her, 'we all get those from

time to time and I have to tell you that's Mark all over
again but life goes on! Come and have your dinner,
there's a good girl—I won't take no for an answer!'
He swung his pony-tail.

Chattie hesitated, feeling a bit like Alice about to
sup at a Mad Hatter's dinner but also conscious that
now was the time to clear up the confusion. She
opened her mouth but Steve stood up and looked down
at her with a glint of mockery.

'I'm not susceptible to girls going into a decline
over my brother,' he said.

She got up and if looks could have killed Steve
Kinane would have toppled to the floor. If anything,
though, her flashing look seemed to amuse him and
he said quite gently, 'After you.' He gestured. 'I'll
bring the wine.'

She had no idea what prompted her to do it but she
swished past him and walked into the dining room
proudly. To show him she was not to be trifled with?
she wondered. But at the same time she got the uncomfortable feeling she'd attracted his attention in a
way she'd rather not—it was almost as if his dark eyes
were boring into her back.

She swung round as she reached the table and their
gazes clashed. To her mortification, she detected more
amusement as well as appreciation in his—appreciation of her figure. Then he looked away and picked
up the wine.

She ground her teeth at the same time as a strange
little sensation ran through her but she didn't have the
time to identify it—Slim was holding a chair out
for her.

In the event, she turned out to be hungrier than she'd thought. Either that or Slim's dinner was irresistible— Parma ham and melon followed by roast beef and Yorkshire pudding.

It was while she was tucking into the roast beef that Steve said, 'Tell me a bit more about yourself, Chattie. Were you born in Brisbane? Are your parents alive?'

She paused to take a sip of wine and told him the bare bones of her life story.

'That's rather unusual,' Steve commented.

Chattie neatly dissected a piece of beef and dabbed some mustard on it, but offered no further information.

'And you've lived in Brisbane all your life?'

The next bite she ate was a piece of Yorkshire pudding. 'Slim obviously knows his stuff; this is very good.'

'Slim does know his stuff. Why wouldn't you want me to know your background, Chattie?'

Grey eyes encountered dark brown ones.

'I can't see why my background is of any interest to you,' she said at last. 'I have no interest in yours.'

'I'm devastated.' Steve Kinane continued to eat his dinner without the least sign of devastation, however.

Chattie eyed a fine grandfather clock with a gold moon rising on its blue face, then finished her meal in silence.

Steve did the same and Slim appeared right on cue bearing a platter of cheese and fruit. 'Coffee's on its way,' he said.

Steve reached for a peach and started to peel it. His hands, she noticed again, despite her state of mind, were callused and strong but long, lean and scrubbed clean now. For some reason, it started her thinking along another tack…

She looked around. Some of it might be old-fashioned but there was an awful lot of substance to Mount Helena homestead. In fact, as her gaze travelled from painting to painting on the green-papered walls of the dining room and her eyes widened in recognition, some of that substance could be priceless. Then there was the china and crystal—she tapped a nail against her wineglass and the ping of crystal, Stuart, she guessed, resounded.

She resisted the temptation to turn over her side plate but thought the colourful, ornate, gilded and scrolled dinner service might be Rockingham or Coalport. The tablecloth was definitely fine white damask.

Her gaze returned to the grandfather clock but her mind's eye presented her with the vehicle Steve Kinane drove; dusty it might have been, but it was also a late model four-wheel drive with 'all the trimmings'.

She had not, she realized as all this impressed itself on her, given Mark Kinane's background a lot of thought. Now she was forced to wonder if it was very wealthy and that was why Steve Kinane was on his guard about girls running after his apparently profligate brother.

'So?'

She jumped and turned her head to Steve. 'So—what?'

'I gather you were making some assessments, checking the silver, testing the crystal and so on.'

She coloured faintly but answered evenly, '*I* gather your brother would be quite a catch?'

'He would. Have some grapes and cheese.'

Chattie took a bunch of grapes but studied the bloom on them instead of eating them. 'Is that why you feel entitled to police his love life?'

The air became literally electric between them. She saw the spark of anger in his eyes and the way his mouth hardened. In fact she quaked inwardly with fright but refused to allow herself to look away.

'You are a cool one, aren't you?' he drawled at last. 'No, I don't police his love life. What I do take exception to are girls "on the make", girls who succumb to unplanned pregnancies in the hope of trapping him into marriage—and the like. I do hope you're not about to tell me you're one of those, Miss Winslow?'

Chattie drew a deep breath as his eyes challenged her insolently, and all hope of explaining Bridget's predicament and getting a fair hearing flew out of the window.

So what to do now? she wondered. Go back home and tell her sister to forget about Mark Kinane because they'd never get past his definitely dictatorial if not to say dangerous brother Steve? Or hang in in whatever way she, Chattie, could until she found some way of getting in touch with Mark?

The thought resolved itself into speech almost simultaneously and was backed by a deep well of anger against this man.

'You need have no qualms on that score, Mr Kinane. I'm not pregnant. At the same time, whether you believe you're policing Mark's love life or not, there's no way you can police me, and I don't intend to leave here until I find out where Mark is.'

The silence reverberated with all the shivering strands of their mutual animosity. Heightened, Chattie found herself wondering suddenly, by their mutual curiosity about each other?

Then the sound of a motor intruded, and a squeal of tyres as a vehicle slammed to a stop outside. A little pulse of hope stirred within Chattie—that it was Mark Kinane.

But the person who pounded through the hall and into the lounge as Steve put his napkin down and rose was a girl, a girl in the grip of strong emotion, at that.

'Steve, you *won't* believe this,' she began as she saw him in the dining room, 'Jack's walked out on me! The two-timing bastard's done it again but if he thinks he's going to get away with it, he's mistaken.' She paused, panting, and her eyes fell on Chattie.

At the same time a boy of about six wandered into the lounge with his thumb in his mouth and a teddy bear tucked under his arm. He took no notice of anyone but climbed onto a settee and curled up as if sleeping wherever and whenever he could find a spot came quite naturally to him.

'For heaven's sake, Harriet,' Steve said in a grim undertone, 'couldn't you have rung rather than dragging Brett out at this time of night?'

Harriet opened her mouth, stopped, then, with an imperious jerk of her head, indicated Chattie. 'Who the hell is this?'

Chattie felt herself bridle instinctively. Whoever *she* was, this Harriet was a tall girl with an attitude. She had cropped chestnut hair, freckles, piercing blue eyes and her hands-on-hips stance indicated a belligerent nature, causing Chattie to feel some sympathy for the unknown Jack.

'This is Chattie Winslow,' Steve said. 'She's just passing through. Harriet—'

But Harriet burst into tears.

Steve Kinane raised his eyes to the ceiling and walked over to the liquor cabinet where he poured a tot of brandy.

'Here.' He led Harriet to a chair at the dining table. 'Drink this,' he said, not unkindly.

Harriet took a sip, then proceeded to pour out a disjointed tale of woe.

Chattie found herself rooted to the spot by the whole extraordinary rigmarole and the contradictions that emerged. For, at the same time as Harriet hated Jack Barlow passionately, she appeared to be devastated at the thought of losing him. At the same time as he could be the most frustrating husband and Harriet the most misunderstood wife in the world, there was no way any other woman was going to get her hooks into him...

Brett slept through it all but finally the flow was stemmed somewhat and Harriet raised drenched blue eyes to Steve. 'You do see that I have to go after him, don't you?' she said intensely.

He paused, and Chattie got the feeling Steve Kinane didn't see that at all but knew when he was fighting against thunder. 'Not right now, tomorrow morning will do,' he said finally.

'But—'

'No, Harriet,' he overrode her. 'If you want to leave Brett with me and Slim, that's the condition.'

Harriet hesitated, then got up and flung her arms around her him. 'You're a brick, Steve,' she told him. 'Mind if I sleep here tonight?'

He shook his head.

And, completely ignoring Chattie, Harriet scooped her offspring off the settee and waltzed out with him.

Chattie watched her go and blinked several times.

'I know, it's like being visited by a tornado.' Steve looked wry.

'I'm not sure if she loves him or hates him,' Chattie said involuntarily, then put her hand to her mouth as Slim came in with a tray of coffee. 'Pardon me, it has nothing to do with me.'

'She's besotted,' Slim said severely, 'but I've never known anyone with less tact or more capable of picking a fight than she is and the only way Jack can handle it at times is to run away. Excuse me, I'll go and make sure she has all she needs.'

Steve Kinane grimaced as his housekeeper departed, and Chattie had to chuckle at his expression.

'I would say Slim knows you all very well,' she said humorously.

For the life of him, Steve Kinane couldn't resist the glint of humour in those lovely grey eyes. 'He's the ultimate authority,' he replied ruefully, then shrugged. 'Harriet is a cousin but she lived with us after her parents separated so she's more like a sister. Jack is the station foreman and they have their own house on another part of the property.' His gaze narrowed on her then. 'Obviously Mark didn't tell you about her?'

Chattie shook her head as she got the feeling that the brief respite in their hostilities was over.

She was right. Steve Kinane joined his hands behind

his head and studied her expressionlessly but comprehensively.

To cover her nerves, she murmured, 'Why don't I be mother?' She picked up the silver coffee pot.

He let her pour the coffee, then added sugar but no milk to his.

Chattie did likewise and inhaled the fragrant aroma appreciatively.

'There's no way you can stay here against my wishes, Miss Winslow,' he said grimly.

'What about Mark's wishes?' she murmured. 'Do you ignore them entirely?'

'Since Mark neglected to advise me of any wishes at all in regard to you, I feel quite entitled to ignore them, whatever they are. I'm not even sure any exist,' he added.

'Look, I do know your brother and I'm perfectly entitled to…want to look him up,' she said evenly.

'How old are you?' he shot back.

She blinked. 'Twenty-two but why do you need to know?'

'I get the feeling you're too old for Mark,' he drawled.

'Well, as you now know, I'm not. We're the same age.'

He ignored that. 'How come you're sashaying around the countryside when you should be teaching little girls to cook and sew? Unless you're masquerading as a domestic science teacher?'

Chattie took a deep breath. 'I don't only teach girls, it's a TAFE college, adult education in other words, and we're on holiday at present.'

Steve Kinane formed one hand into a fist and laid

it on the table. 'That's the other thing—you just don't seem to be his type. Level-headed and domesticated are not what he usually goes for.'

'If that's a diplomatic way of saying I'm—' she paused and amended herself, Make that my sister! '—not *good* enough for your brother—'

'I didn't say that,' he broke in.

Chattie plaited her fingers and reproved herself for starting to lose her temper. She also found herself almost unbearably tempted to come clean with Mark's brother before this got any further out of hand.

However, he said then, musingly, 'No, if anything you're too good to be true. Because Mark, to date anyway, has always fallen for models, aspiring actresses or glamorous young things who would be totally at sea out here with no shops, no restaurants, no hairdressers and so on.'

Chattie bit her lip and felt her stomach sink. Despite the Rockingham, the Stuart crystal and the fortune on the walls, from what she'd seen of the countryside she couldn't doubt it would be an isolated lifestyle devoid of—as he'd just catalogued—just about everything that made up Bridget's life.

On the other hand, if Mark and Bridget decided they had a future together, would it have to be at Mount Helena? His own brother had, not that long ago, made mention of the fact that Mark and the station only went together in small doses.

'Got you there, Miss Winslow?'

Chattie came out of her reverie to find him smiling lethally at her.

'What you seem to misunderstand, persistently, is that Mark is a friend I'm trying to look up.'

'Bulldust,' he said softly. 'You're worried about something, Miss Winslow. You got much more of a shock than a mere acquaintance would have got to find he'd gone.'

Chattie cursed herself inwardly for being so transparent. At the same time, all desire to come clean with Steve Kinane left her as she made the decision that she would do anything she had to do to get her hands on his brother and not only for her sister's sake but just to annoy him…

'All right.' She shrugged. 'Let me put my cards on the table. Not quite in the backhanded way you've put it but, all the same, we seem to be in some agreement. I think I'd be good for Mark. And—' she looked around '—I prefer a challenging lifestyle over restaurants, hairdressers, shops and so on.'

For a moment his expression defied description.

'Got you there, Mr Kinane?'

What he would have said and done, she was never to know because Slim, with Rich pattering along behind, came into the room.

The dog grinned widely at Chattie, accorded Steve a brief glance and sat down at her feet to lay his nose adoringly on her knee.

'This is quite some dog, Miss Winslow,' Slim said. 'He's very well-mannered.'

'But just as capable of eating anyone alive,' Steve remarked acidly.

Slim laughed. 'You're not wrong. Had one myself years ago that nearly landed me in jail. Tore the pants off a policeman, he did! By the way, Mrs Barlow and young Master Barlow are asleep.'

'Thank you, Slim,' Steve said. 'I'm about to turn in

myself. Two nights at the bore camp, not to mention Miss Winslow's company, have quite worn me out.' He stood up. 'Please feel free to do whatever you would like to,' he said to Chattie, 'bar nicking any of the silver, and please be ready to depart straight after breakfast tomorrow. Goodnight.'

Slim watched him go with his hands on his hips, then began to clear the table. 'I wouldn't take that too much to heart,' he said to Chattie, still frozen to her chair. 'He has a lot of responsibilities.'

'I don't intend to,' she replied, 'but I've never met anyone as…' She paused, lost for words.

'Well, Mark flitting off into the wild blue yonder obviously hasn't improved his mood. There's a muster coming up, there's all sorts of things coming up, guests and what not, and not only has Mark done a bunk, so has Jack Barlow.' Slim shook his head. 'But Steve's OK, you know.'

Chattie rose. 'I'm not in the position to agree with you but I'd like to thank you for your hospitality, Slim. Can I give you hand?'

Although Slim looked gratified, and for a moment almost assessing, as if something had popped into his mind that had surprised him, he didn't reveal it and declined her offer.

'You pop off to bed,' he advised, 'but thanks all the same!'

CHAPTER THREE

AT TWO o'clock, the next morning, Chattie was wide awake beneath a sea of red silk quilt.

Rich was asleep on his favourite rug beside the bed and the house was quiet apart from the roof contracting in the cool night air with a series of creaks.

Not only was she wide awake but she was far from feeling serene as her mind's eye presented her with a recap of the previous day. In fact, her stomach was in knots as she contemplated all that had led up to her looking down the barrel of being booted off Mount Helena station.

Somehow or other, she had to discover Mark Kinane's whereabouts before that happened, but she had not the faintest idea how to go about it. If they didn't know where he was what hope did she have?

Also, it was all very well to, in the heat of the moment, take Steve Kinane head-on, but it was playing havoc with her nerves and her digestion. It had a distinctly 'playing with fire' feel to it, she acknowledged, and if it weren't for Bridget to fuel her defences and ingenuity, she would probably be only too grateful to be removed from his line of sight.

One thing she was sure of—that the curious frisson she'd experienced a couple of times beneath the onslaught of his looks and masculinity had been hammered to death by so many things he'd said or implied but the final blow had to be the 'nicking the silver' taunt.

She flinched as she recalled the mockery in his dark eyes as he'd said it, and anger started to seep through her veins again. Anger plus some of her famed—or would that be notorious? she wondered—level-headedness. Did they really not know Mark's whereabouts? Or was it a front?

Then it occurred to her that she had some sort of an ally in Slim. At least, she got the feeling that, for reasons best known to himself, Slim didn't share his boss's outright disapproval of her and, not that it came naturally to her to snoop, might she be able to get more information from the housekeeper?

After all, she told herself, she had been virtually pilloried as a girl on the make; a girl who'd deliberately got herself pregnant to trap Mark; a girl dubious enough to be warned against pinching the silver, so why should she bother about observing the niceties towards Steve Kinane?

It was also the only thing she could come up with, she thought forlornly.

By the time Chattie got up the next morning and presented herself for breakfast, there was no sign of Harriet or Steve.

Breakfast, she discovered, was served in the vast kitchen. A bright, airy room, it overlooked the water tanks with their cloak of pink, purple and rusty bougainvillaea and yellow allamanda. It was also a cook's delight with cork-tiled floors, a wrought-iron pot-holder hanging from the ceiling and a butcher's chopping block on wheels.

There were herbs in pots on the window sill, a scullery that led off it and a big round table in an alcove set with chunky, colourful china.

Her companion at the table was Brett, stirring a bowl of oatmeal with little enthusiasm and swinging his legs at the same time.

Slim looked over his shoulder from the wood fire stove. 'Morning, miss. Sleep well?'

Chattie tipped a hand. 'On and off. Then I fell into this deep sleep and that's why I'm a bit later than normal.'

'Never mind! Sit down. What's your preference? Help yourself to juice, by the way.'

Seeing that he was tending bacon, sausages and eggs, she asked for one sausage and an egg, and poured herself some orange juice.

'Who are you?' Brett enquired. 'And why don't you have to have porridge?'

'Because I'm all grown up,' Chattie replied. 'When you're growing, porridge is an excellent body-builder.'

Brett rolled his eyes. 'That's what they say about nearly all the things I don't like. Are you Steve's girlfriend?'

'I am definitely *not* Steve's girlfriend,' Chattie said with emphasis at the same time as Steve Kinane appeared in the back doorway.

He pulled his boots off, tossed his broad-brimmed hat onto a hook on the wall and strolled over to the table in his socks. He looked big and there was something bracing about his presence. There was also something a little breathtaking about the width of his shoulders, his height and the way his dark hair flopped onto his forehead.

'That would be a fate worse than death,' he commented to Brett. 'Morning, Chattie.' Their gazes clashed and his was full of mockery but a different kind of mockery as once again he mentally stripped her.

'What does that mean?' Brett asked immediately.

Chattie had looked away in some confusion but she now turned back to Steve and surrendered the floor to him with a touch of malice in her eyes.

'It means…' Steve poured himself orange juice '…that—'

'It means,' Slim said severely as he placed a plate in front of Chattie, 'that these two don't quite see eye to eye, that's all. Brett, old son, if you don't finish that soon I will…' He paused, placed a hand over his heart, and keeled over onto the floor.

In their scramble to get to him, Steve knocked over his juice and Chattie's plate of sausage and egg went flying.

'What? What's wrong with him?' Chattie breathed, taking in the blue tinge to Slim's skin as she knelt beside him.

'He's got a dicky heart. Bring me the phone!' Steve commanded.

She glanced around wildly then spied what looked like a remote phone with an antenna on the kitchen counter. 'Here.' She pushed it into Steve's hand. 'Look, I know how to do CPR—'

'Good, you start it while I raise the flying doctor.'

An hour and a half later the three of them, Steve, Chattie and Brett, watched the flying doctor take off from the station's airstrip with Slim on board.

'Is he going to die?' Brett asked tearfully.

'Don't think so,' Steve said, 'but anyway he's in really good hands now.' He picked Brett up and put him on his shoulders for the short stroll back to the house.

'I don't like what happened, it made me really scared,' Brett said in his high, piping voice—and they stopped as an excited bark came from the direction of the house.

Chattie put a hand to her mouth. 'Rich! I forgot about him. Apart from a walk earlier he's been locked up on the veranda.'

'You've got a dog?' Brett queried alertly.

'Yes. Would you like to see him?'

Steve changed direction towards the guest bedroom veranda and put Brett down. He immediately raced towards the veranda.

'Rich adores kids,' Chattie said. 'And he might just distract Brett.'

Events proved exactly that. Rich streaked down the veranda steps as Brett opened the gate, flung himself up at Chattie briefly, ignored Steve totally, and then raced back to Brett with obvious delight.

'I see what you mean,' Steve commented.

'It makes my blood boil all over again, to think that anyone could have done that to a dog who gives so much pleasure,' she said.

He looked down at her with a faint frown, as if something was puzzling him about her, but in the end all he said was, 'It is hard to understand. Do you think we deserve a cup of coffee?'

She nodded after a moment.

'Stay here, I'll get it.'

Chattie stared after him, prey to some conflicting emotions. Thanks to his cool control and meticulous following of the flying doctor's instructions before the plane had arrived, Slim had had the best treatment he could have had in the circumstances and now had a good chance of recovery.

And it slid into her mind that Steve Kinane was a good man to have beside you in crisis—unless you happened to hate his guts.

He brought, not only coffee, but also buttered raisin toast to her veranda. Brett and Rich were now playing with a ball on the lawn.

It was a beautiful morning, clear and sunny, not a cloud in the sky and not too hot. She suspected that midsummer would be very hot at Mount Helena but at the moment, as April slid into May, autumn was a pleasure and the gold-cloaked hills behind the house stood out in such clarity, Chattie longed to have a paintbrush in her fingers.

'That's one problem in hand,' he said as he poured the coffee.

Chattie brought her mind back from the landscape. 'Brett?' she hazarded. 'I gather Harriet has already left?'

'At the crack of dawn.'

'What will you do?'

He studied her over the rim of his cup. She wore jeans and a blue blouse and her hair was plaited to one side. After her initial shock, she'd been both practical and very helpful with Slim and in dealing with Brett. Was that any reason to be contemplating what he was contemplating out of the blue, however? It just

didn't make sense to ask her to stay on for a while—
or, on one level, at least, did it? The level that this
mysterious girl intrigued him...

'My life,' he observed carefully after a long moment, 'has suddenly become extremely complicated. I
have no housekeeper, Brett has no parents, I'm minus
a station foreman as well as my brother and all in the
space of less than twenty-four hours.'

Chattie bit into a piece of toast and frowned but
said nothing.

'How much of your school holidays have you got
to go?' he asked then.

His intentions began to dawn on Chattie and she
took a sudden breath. 'Uh—just over three weeks.'

'You did tell me you were a girl of many domesticated talents. Not to put too fine a point on it, you
could help me out of a bit of a hole, Chattie Winslow,
but don't,' he said as she opened her mouth to speak,
'imagine it would be a one way street. I would be
more than happy to pay for your time.'

'Just what are you offering me?' she asked suspiciously.

'A temporary position as Slim's replacement.'

She chewed her lip.

'You did come up here to see a working cattle station, didn't you?'

'Yes. But...' She trailed off disjointedly for the
good reason that she was thinking furiously. Had the
opportunity to stay on until she discovered where
Mark was simply fallen into her lap?

'What's the difference?' He raised his eyebrows
ironically.

'Mark would have been here, should have been

here,' she said at last, then continued with more composure. 'It is completely different. I don't know *you* from a bar of soap—'

'Oh, come on, surely the old bar of soap doesn't wash,' he said with a tinge of impatience. 'You've had dinner with me, met my crazy cousin, you know my brother as you keep telling me—and you've just helped me to save someone's life.'

She hesitated as she wondered how to play it. Too much eagerness might arouse his already heightened suspicions of her... In the end she opted for, 'I don't like you. You don't like me.'

His lips twisted. 'It wouldn't be for long and I'm not suggesting we go to bed together, merely that you do a bit of housekeeping for me.'

Her eyes flashed, causing him to smile faintly.

She put down her plate and reached for her coffee. 'Aren't you worried about me pinching the silver?'

'No—'

'You were last night.'

'That was—' he looked amused '—a shot designed to annoy you more than the conviction you were a thief. And who knows?' he added idly. 'Mark might even turn up.'

The silence stretched as Chattie battled with her nervous tension at the thought of living with and working for this man, and weighed it against the possibility of securing her sister's future in some way.

'I pay well,' Steve Kinane added idly.

'What makes you think that's a consideration with me,' she asked with hauteur.

He shrugged. 'Just thought I'd mention it to reinforce the fact that we're talking about a business agreement.'

She eyed him. 'How much?'

He named a weekly figure, which, considering her food and board were all found, was astonishing.

'Is that how much you paid Slim?' she asked incredulously.

'No, I paid him more but he's been doing the job for the last five years since this heart condition has kept him out of the saddle so he's very experienced. Getting good staff out here is not that easy.'

She finished her coffee.

'Then again,' he drawled, 'I'd quite understand if you didn't feel up to the position. There is a bit more to it than appears on the surface.'

'Like what?'

'Let's see, I have a house party due to descend on Helena shortly, five people here for two nights, that's quite a bit of cooking and housework, and one meal is a formal dinner for ten. That kind of thing.'

'And you think I couldn't cope with that?' She raised her chin.

He shrugged. 'I'm asking you.'

'I could do it with my eyes shut,' she told him tartly, 'but on one condition.'

'Name it,' he murmured.

'If, at any time while I'm here, you find out where Mark is, I get to know too.'

Determined grey eyes engaged dark brown ones and the atmosphere between them couldn't have been more fraught if they'd been engaged in a duel.

Then Steve Kinane said flatly, 'Are you really madly in love with him?'

Chattie chose her words with care. 'That's none of your business. Do we have a deal?'

Something flickered in Steve's dark eyes. 'If he's driving to Broome—'

'He's driving? All the way to Broome?' Chattie interrupted. 'That's nearly right across the continent.'

'Yep.' He got up. 'But we country people are used to driving long distances. And I'm only assuming he's driving to Broome but, if he is, he'll be out of mobile range a lot of the time.'

'All the same, wouldn't he…' Chattie hesitated '…have more sophisticated equipment with him other than a mobile phone for such a long trip?'

'What did you have in mind?'

She gestured. 'A satellite phone?'

'Have you any idea how much satellite phones cost?'

'No, but you seem to have everything else that opens and shuts.'

He smiled satanically. 'How would you know?'

'Well, that phone you used to get in touch with the flying doctor—'

'Was a satellite phone,' he conceded, 'but it's kept for emergencies. Not…' he paused and continued with patent irony '…for Mark's personal use in sorting out his love life.'

Chattie came to her feet rather like a spring uncoiling as she was hit by Bridget's conviction that the root cause of all Mark's problems was this insufferable man. 'Has it ever occurred to you that Mark may have benefited from a less "superior" older brother, Mr Kinane?'

They eyed each other.

'He really did get you in, didn't he?' he said at last.

'He really did get me in, yes,' Chattie agreed, although she crossed her fingers behind her back and assured herself all was fair in this kind of war.

'So it's no good me telling you I've done my level best to steer Mark down the right road ever since he left school?'

'None at all,' she answered with dry economy.

He cocked his head to one side and frowned. 'Apart from the obvious—why is that?'

'What would the obvious be?' Chattie enquired.

'His skills in bed,' he drawled and ran his gaze up and down her body. 'Something, incidentally, I have no doubt he's very good at.'

Chattie went white. 'How dare you?'

He lifted an eyebrow. 'I can't imagine in the limited time you've known him that you've been able to assess his other qualities too accurately.'

For some insane reason, it occurred to Chattie to wonder how good Steve Kinane was in bed. She had no doubt he was a man's man, she had no doubt he was tough and strong, that he was also cool-headed under pressure and commanding at times, but was there another side to him?

From the way he was looking at her, she suddenly couldn't doubt that there was. His dark appraisal of her had all the hallmarks of a man who knew women well enough to be forming some opinions on how good *she* was in bed. The mere thought of it made her go hot and cold and feel quite panicky—why on earth was she thinking along these lines about a man she barely knew, even visualising his strong hands on her body with an inward little tremor?

'There is one quality I'm familiar with,' she said, wrenching her mind away from the unbelievable. 'He is not a dyed-in-the-wool grazier as you appear to be and forcing him to spend his life here when he hates it is diabolical.'

Steve Kinane folded his arms and, to Chattie's utter surprise, laughed softly. 'Is that what he told you?'

She gritted her teeth. 'Yes.'

'Then let me set the record straight, Miss Winslow. Mark is free to do what he likes. But if he expects Mount Helena to support him—and to date he's come up with no other visible means of support—then I expect *him* to put his shoulder to the wheel when he's needed. What's so unreasonable about that?'

Chattie gripped her hands together and took a deep breath. 'Families are still families even if they're going through trying times, even if they're much younger and seem to lack direction,' she said with quiet passion.

Surprise caused Steve's eyes to widen then narrow.

'The other thing is,' she went on, 'although I haven't experienced being old yet, I'm sure it's all too easy to forget what it's like to be young.'

He opened his mouth, closed it, then said incredulously, 'How bloody old do you think I am?'

'Thirty-two since Mark is twenty-two and you're about ten years older.'

'And you think that's *old*?'

She shook her head. 'Not so much in years but it can also be a state of mind.'

Fortunately, perhaps, Brett chose that moment to return to the veranda with Rich. 'We're hungry,' he announced.

'Just as well there's some raisin toast left,' Chattie said, and handed Brett a slice. 'I don't think Rich likes—oh, yes, he does!' she added with a gurgle of laughter as Rich pinched a piece of toast. 'Let's hope—' she raised her eyes to Steve '—this doesn't mean Brett will develop a liking for dog food!'

Steve Kinane had to smile but it was a perfunctory one as he grappled with the distinct feeling that Chattie Winslow had got the better of him. Not only that, as he watched her bend down to the dog and the boy, the more he got to know her, the more gorgeous she appeared to him. Dressed up or dressed down didn't seem to make much difference, her hips in blue denim were a delight…and therein could lie a problem for him.

A lovely body but the mind of an amateur philosopher, not to mention in love with his brother, he reminded himself ruefully—what could be more of a disaster for him?

Chattie straightened, and saw something in Steve Kinane's eyes as they rested on her again that was infinitely disturbing—why should the dark gaze of this man be so compelling? Wasn't she equally convinced that he was autocratic and insensitive even if he was— sexy?

Then he cut the eye contact. 'If you'd care to come with me,' he said as he turned away, 'we can try to raise Mark now.'

She hesitated but Brett and Rich appeared to be content so she followed him through her bedroom and across the other side of the house to the office.

It was a small, cluttered room with a map of the property on the wall and a battered old roll-top desk.

There was also a table with a computer, what looked to be a single side band radio and a phone.

He reached for a black covered phone book and leafed through it. 'I assume you would have tried his mobile?' he said then and Chattie held her breath because she had asked Bridget about a mobile number for Mark Kinane only to be told he kept losing them so didn't bother with one.

'He…appeared to have lost it,' she said.

Steve slammed the phone book down on the desk. 'Not again! Bloody hell! That must be the sixth one he's lost. I wonder if it's occurred to you that the man you're chasing across the country is almost criminally careless?'

Chattie failed to respond because Bridget was also careless with her keys, her purse—umbrellas were always disappearing, she'd even lost the car they shared in a multi-storey car park and it had taken her two hours to find it.

'What?' Steve Kinane asked.

My sister and your brother, if ever they do get together will either be wonderfully well suited or a disaster, it ran through her mind. 'Uh—nothing,' she said.

'No, it wasn't,' he contradicted irritably. 'Something struck you quite forcibly.'

Chattie lowered her eyes and castigated herself again for being transparent.

'Am I not allowed to be critical of Mark—is that it?' He looked at her incredulously.

She grasped the straw. 'I tried to make that point earlier.'

He said something unprintable, then took hold.

'Look, I have no idea how to get in touch with him, but you have my word, if he checks in I'll tell you. In the meantime, I have a muster to organize; I told you about the house party, I have a parentless kid on my hands—are you going to take the job or not?'

'Yes,' she said slowly, although she added the rider, 'but only for so long as I'm comfortable with it.'

He looked heavenwards but once again reined his feelings in. 'Thank you. By the way, I don't expect you to work yourself to death—if you keep us clean-clothed and fed to start with, I'd appreciate it. Slim did also have some help and…' he paused to listen '…from the sounds I hear in the kitchen, she has arrived. Come and meet Merlene.'

Merlene was in her thirties, well padded, at least six feet tall, she had a spiked haircut and if that didn't give her a belligerent look, her bikie attire and prominent chin did.

Steve passed on the information about Slim and introduced Chattie as his temporary replacement.

Merlene's eyebrows almost disappeared into her hair. 'That was fast work. So his old ticker is playing up again? Darn me.' She subjected Chattie to a thorough inspection and turned back to Steve. 'You serious?'

'Miss Winslow comes highly recommended,' he said gravely. 'All the same, I'd appreciate it if you could give her all the help you can, Merlene. And I'd appreciate it if you'd move into Slim's quarters in the annexe for the time being. In the meantime, I need to get back to work.'

*　*　*

'Here's the gist of it, Chattie,' Merlene said after Steve's departure. 'I do floors, windows, walls, the laundry and ironing and I chop the wood for the stove.'

'That must be an enormous help!'

'I do not,' Merlene continued, 'do bathrooms, I do not dust or polish furniture and knick-knacks, I do not cook or do dishes, and if that's Brett I hear, I do not run around after kids.'

'Naturally,' Chattie said a little faintly, beginning to wilt beneath the force of Merlene's strictures and intense blue gaze.

'Nor do I mend or sew, wait on tables or arrange flowers.'

'That's fine with me. Um—'

'And I do not take kindly to having my work picked over and criticized—which Slim had a nasty habit of doing!'

'I wouldn't dream of it,' Chattie said fervently, having gained the distinct impression that Merlene could pick her up with one hand. Her other thought was that Steve Kinane could have warned her before casting her upon the untender mercies of this woman.

'And—' Merlene pulled out a chair and sat down at the kitchen table '—I don't believe for one minute you're here as a replacement anything. Word has it one of Mark's fancy pieces followed him out to Helena only to find he'd done a bunk to Broome— least-wise that's what we're betting on.' She folded her arms.

Chattie digested this and decided she'd had enough. So she explained that she did know Mark but that was no one's business but her own and she didn't give a damn what anyone thought about her because she was quite secure in the knowledge that she was no one's *fancy* piece.

Merlene unfolded her arms. 'You and me could get along,' she said. 'How about a cuppa? I usually start my working day with one.'

Chattie breathed a little easier. 'Thank you.'

'Then I'll show you the ropes. By the way, I work three hours a day and you don't have to worry about feeding me while I'm sleeping in the annexe, I'll still take my meals down in the bunkhouse with the guys.'

Chattie looked bewildered. 'Why are you sleeping in the annexe, then?'

'Search me,' Merlene replied, then gave the matter some thought. 'I guess Steve likes to do things by the book and you two being alone here at nights mightn't look good.'

'Oh.'

'Although,' Merlene said, with her first flash of humour as she scanned Chattie from head to toe, 'whether it's your reputation he's worried about—or his—is a moot point. Now don't get your dander up! Only joking.'

By lunch time, Chattie had been instructed in all the core functionings of the Mount Helena homestead.

Along the way she'd also gathered snippets of information that fleshed out life on Mount Helena for her and gave her an insight into some of its inhabitants.

Slim and Merlene, for example, were sworn enemies but, she gathered, would probably be bereft without each other to fight.

Merlene herself had lived on Mount Helena all her life and had followed in her ringer father's footsteps until an accident had given her a reason to quit all the dust and toil of it. These days all she rode was her motor bike—much more predictable and better sprung than a horse. As well as her so clearly defined house duties, she operated a store for the workers, of which there were five permanent ones. She was the only woman on Mount Helena other than Harriet Barlow, of whom she had a low opinion.

She also imparted some knowledge to Chattie about the size of Mount Helena and how many head of cattle it ran, information that caused Chattie's eyes to widen.

And when Chattie commented on all the lovely things in the house, she told her that Steve and Mark's mother had been a great lady of great taste.

She didn't have anything to say on the subject of Mark Kinane—hard as it was to conceive, Chattie thought she was being tactful—but there was a definite flavour in her other observations that would have led Chattie to believe—had she not believed otherwise!— that the sun shone out of Steve Kinane.

Then it was one o'clock and Steve came home for lunch.

Mount Helena didn't have a fridge, it had a whole cold room, and out of it Chattie hastily assembled a simple meal of cold beef and salad.

'I'll be able to do better than this tomorrow,' she assured him, poured him a cup of tea and started to cut up Brett's beef for him. 'It's just that Merlene has been kind enough to—really show me the ropes.'

'This is fine,' he murmured. 'No calls?'

'No.'

'So you and Merlene hit it off?' he queried with his lips twisting.

'No thanks to you!'

'Nothing I could say would have made any difference.'

'I don't know about that.' Chattie sat down and smiled at him delightfully. 'I get the feeling you're the blue-eyed boy around here.'

'But you don't have to agree?' he hazarded.

'Bingo!'

'Chattie—' he laughed '—I am not an ogre.'

'What's that?' Brett asked.

'A scary person,' Chattie said.

'Mum says he can be,' Brett contributed. 'Mum says the only person she'd really rather not get on the wrong side of is Steve. Dad said he was amazed to hear it.'

Chattie shot Steve an I-told-you-so look.

But Brett continued, 'I can't see that he's worse than anyone else; actually I think he's a lot better.'

'Thank you, Brett. Do you think you could be parted from Rich long enough to come out into the paddocks with me this afternoon?' Steve asked.

Brett jumped up in his chair. 'Yes, sirree!'

'That way Chattie can have a bit of time to rest and recover her good humour.'

They gazed at each other until Chattie looked away and said stiffly, 'Thank you. I appreciate that. I haven't even unpacked yet,' she added with some amazement.

'By the way, please feel free to play the piano.'

Her eyes widened. 'Thank you again, but I haven't seen one.'

'The music room is off the dining room.' Steve finished his meal, drained his teacup and stood up. 'Let's go, young man.'

That was how, since Merlene had already left noisily on her bike, Chattie came to be alone in the homestead, apart from Rich, and able, for the first time, to think articulately about the surprising about-turn of events.

She poured herself another cup of tea and considered the fact that, whatever fix Steve Kinane found himself in, she would have thought one Chattie Winslow would be the last person he'd turn to for help.

Of course it was quite a fix but he could have contacted a pastoral employment agency, one would have thought, and have someone flown in. So, what did it have to do with her, personally?

She put her cup down and moved restlessly. Contrary to her 'certain sureness', a phrase she and Bridget had used as kids, that she could no longer feel one smidgeon of attraction towards Steve Kinane, there was still something there, to her amazement, something angry but electric at times.

Or was he, as his brother apparently was, a man who couldn't help sending out sensual vibes to any passable woman? Maybe it ran in the family, she mused. In which case, why was she responding? It didn't make sense. OK, he might be dynamic, but he could also be lethally insulting. He was also virtually hogging the high moral ground on the subject of his brother's love life, so…

She shook her head and got up to clear the lunch things and stack the dishwasher.

Then, in a bid to distract herself from all the things

she didn't understand, she went to find the piano. The door from the dining room to the music room was closed. She opened it gingerly—and gasped with delight.

The piano was a black baby grand in a perfect setting. It stood in the middle of the room. French windows with white curtains opened onto a side veranda and there was one divine armchair covered in navy velvet with a matching footstool. Like the dining room, the walls were covered with paintings but these were all vibrant, exotic ones of fruit and flowers, trees, gardens and birds.

A rosewood desk stood against one wall and another wall had built-in shelves laden with silver-framed photos interspersed between books and some lovely *objets d'art*.

It came to her from nowhere as she looked around that this had been the lady of the house's private retreat, and that lady had to have been Mark and Steve's mother, a lady she was starting to feel curious about.

She walked over to the instrument and lifted the lid. The keys were yellow and some of the ivories thin with much use but the tone, as she struck several, as clear as a bell.

She sat down on the stool, also upholstered in navy velvet, and played an air from Handel's 'Water Music', noting as her hands moved up and down that one B flat was a little stiff but otherwise it was the best piano she'd ever played.

She took her hands away from the keys and laid them in her lap as she looked around again, and came to a rather surprising decision. While she was in charge of the well-being of this house, she would take the opportunity to show Steve Kinane that she wasn't too good to be true.

Then she went to find her own mobile phone, and she spent the next ten minutes talking to Bridget and passing on a limited version of what had happened.

CHAPTER FOUR

STEVE dropped Brett off at five o'clock and told Chattie he had a few more things to do but would be back in time for dinner at seven.

Rich was ecstatic about being reunited with the boy, and Chattie let them play for a while. Then she insisted Brett had a bath and, perceiving signs of tiredness in Harriet Barlow's otherwise easygoing son, she gave him an early dinner, read him a story and put him to bed. He fell asleep immediately.

'Well, considering you don't really know me from a bar of soap—to use a well-worn phrase—and your parents have some strange ways,' she murmured with her finger on the light switch, 'you're an amazingly well-behaved child.'

'He is, isn't he?'

She turned to find Steve standing behind her. 'Oh! I didn't hear you come in.'

He studied her for a moment, then, 'Give me ten minutes and I'll be ready for dinner.' He turned away.

'Take as long as you like,' she recommended. 'It'll keep.'

But he was as good as his word.

'I hope this is all right,' she said as he came into the kitchen where she'd set the table for two. 'Merlene told me when it was only family that you eat in here.'

'It's fine. Care for a beer? Or a glass of wine?'

She looked surprised.

'Slim and I generally have a beer.'

'In that case, thank you, I'll have a glass of wine. Have you heard how he is?'

'Yes, I just rang the base hospital. He's resting comfortably but they've decided to fly him to Brisbane for a bypass operation.'

She digested this while she served up the soup and he got the drinks. She'd found some vegetable stock, added some cooked chicken she'd also found, some herbs and at the last minute swirled cream through it. And she placed a basket of crusty rolls she'd made in the bread machine on the table.

'Very good,' Steve Kinane said of the soup. 'That certainly didn't come out of a tin.'

'Is that what you were expecting?' she asked incredulously.

'My apologies to the cook,' he replied wryly. 'It is only your first day.'

'Well—' she got up to remove the soup bowls '—Slim has to take a lot of the credit. He has a very well-organized larder. I do hope you like curry?' She looked at him expectantly.

Steve took his time. She'd changed from her jeans into a three-quarter-length floral skirt and a white blouse. Her hair was tied back and she looked fresh and attractive. Also very slim about the waist, he noted, and wondered how he was going to broach the subject that still bothered him...

'Uh, yes, I do,' he said.

'Good,' she said briskly and moved away from the table. 'I make a mean curry. Not that I've made this one as hot as I can make them, just in case you're a mild curry person, but it should still be good.'

'You like a hot curry?' he queried.

She came back from the scullery and gestured with both hands outstretched. 'Love it.' Then she pirouetted towards the stove and began to dish up her curry.

Is it unconscious? Steve Kinane asked himself. Is she unaware that she has a lovely figure and does she swing her hips quite naturally because she's happy at the moment—or full of annoyed hauteur as she was last night—or is she perfectly aware of the effect she has on men?

Chattie turned from the stove with her eyebrows raised, to intercept his assessing gaze.

'You don't really like curry at all?' she asked with a suddenly and comically anxious expression.

He looked away. 'On the contrary, I also like it hot.'

He started to uncover the sambals already assembled on the table.

She paused, as if testing the air. As if she knew the atmosphere between them was about more than curry but she couldn't put her finger on it.

'My curry,' he murmured, but wondered at the same time what she would make of it if she could read his mind, which had flashed him a mental image of taking her to his bed and exploring every lovely inch of her in a way that would render things very hot between them.

She relaxed with a laugh. 'Wish I'd known!' She turned back to the stove.

His gaze narrowed on her back and he examined another question mark that had risen in his mind. This morning, he'd assured himself that to be attracted to a girl who was in love with his brother was the height of unwisdom. But was it happening whether he liked it or not, even when he wasn't sure he could trust her?

Would he be contemplating hot, steamy sex with her otherwise? he asked himself cynically. And was he imagining it or was she not entirely immune from his physical appreciation of her?

'You're right, it's very good,' he said some time later as he forked up some perfectly cooked, fluffy rice. 'You also seem to be in a very good mood, Chattie.'

Her eyes widened, then she looked wary as she remembered she should be posing as Mark's, possibly abandoned, girlfriend. 'I shouldn't be, I know. I guess I lost myself in my cooking.'

Steve Kinane went to broach one of the subjects he had on his mind but the phone rang, and Chattie sat up expectantly.

He took the call on the kitchen extension but it was Harriet.

'Are they—reconciled?' Chattie asked as he came back to the table.

He shrugged. 'They're talking, at least.'

'You didn't mention Slim,' she pointed out.

'Deliberately. In the event that Harriet felt she had to hare home before it's all resolved so we'd have to go through it all over again. Brett's no trouble, is he?'

'No. Not at all. Actually I like having kids around. He seems to be pretty keen on you.' She pushed her plate away and propped her chin on her hands. 'So I gather you like kids, too?'

'I like Brett, anyway.'

'Can I ask you something?'

He nodded.

She thought for a moment, unwilling to return to what was such a controversial issue between them, but it was concerning her. 'It seems an awful long way away for a fiancée to live, western Queensland to Broome, W.A.' She folded her napkin into a triangle.

'They met at university in Darwin. Mark got a place there he couldn't get in Queensland and, in Bryony's case, Darwin is closer than Perth.'

'Oh.'

'Chattie,' Steve said and paused for a moment to watch her carefully, 'is there something you haven't told me?'

Her lashes lifted. 'Like what?'

He finished his beer and twirled the glass in his fingers. 'You denied last night that you were pregnant, but is it true?' He raised his eyes to hers.

She swallowed as she wondered whether it was an opportunity to put Bridget's case and meet a rational response—but the events of the previous evening were too close to allow her to take the risk. 'No. I mean, no, I'm not pregnant.'

'Are you sure?'

'Of course I'm sure,' she said as colour rushed into her cheeks to think of him considering the state of her body in this light.

'Accidents do happen,' he said with irony.

'I'm sure they do.' She couldn't help herself from making the point with some emphasis and, on an impulse, added, 'If I were pregnant to Mark, what would you do?'

'Chattie—' his gaze was suddenly harsh '—it certainly won't help things if you've been lying to me.'

'I'm not,' she said quietly, but very conscious that

she was, in a way. Then she frowned. 'Why do you seem to be so concerned about it?'

'I couldn't help wondering if it was why you wanted to speak to Mark so desperately.'

She stared at him.

'Because,' he added, 'if I'd received the news you had, I don't think I'd have been that keen to speak to him at all. I mean, to all intents and purposes, he had a bit of a fling with you, invited you up here, then forgot all about it and took off.'

She folded her napkin into a smaller triangle. 'I see. Well, it's not that I'm pregnant but, speaking theoretically, how *would* you handle it if it—had happened?'

He smiled dryly. 'I'll cross that bridge when I come to it—if I ever come to it, and I just hope to hell I never do. May I ask you one more time—are you sure?'

More than ever sure I need to find Mark Kinane, she thought, but said, 'I am not pregnant.'

At that moment Merlene's motor bike made itself heard—her unlikely duenna had returned from the bunkhouse.

Chattie rose and added, 'I hope you like sticky date pudding?'

For a second Steve Kinane looked quite menacing, then he started to laugh.

He also said something that startled Chattie.

'I wonder if Mark knows what he's missing out on? Yes, I do like sticky date pudding, Miss Winslow.'

Two days later, Chattie had got quite settled into a routine at Mount Helena, and got to know a bit more about the station.

She was thinking of it as she, Brett and Rich were having a picnic lunch on the lawn under some shady gum-trees. Steve was away for the day, Rich and Brett were playing tirelessly with an old rubber tube and she gazed around, marvelling again at the colours of the landscape and thinking thoughts along the lines of how Mount Helena represented an empire of its own.

Yesterday, Steve had given her a short tour of the bunkhouse, the stables, the cattle yards and the mountain from which the station took its name. It was all impressive; you didn't have to have any experience of a cattle station to appreciate the solid fences, the well-maintained sheds and the expensive machinery they contained, including one helicopter.

Nor could you fail to see that, although Steve Kinane had an easy manner with his staff, he was still very much the boss. And it came to her again that she must have been mad ever to have mistaken him for one of his workers because there was—how to put it?—a touch of class about him?

She paused her thoughts in some surprise as this came to her. Considering the hostility she bore towards him, it was a surprising thought and she tried to gauge where it came from. Not solely to do with looks, she decided. So could it be because of a certain reserve about him that she sensed?

Now she knew him a bit better, he was obviously a more complex person than his brother. Not only that, she now saw that he did bear a lot of responsibility and did it well. He was also, so long as the thorny issue of Mark didn't rise between them, quite easy to get along with.

She plucked a blade of grass, chewed it, and wondered what she would have made of Steve Kinane in different circumstances...

'How was your day?'

'Fine, thanks,' Chattie said to Steve as she brought a chicken casserole to the table for dinner that evening. 'How was yours?'

'Complicated.' He lifted the lid on the casserole and sniffed appreciatively. 'I'm so under-staffed at the moment, I may have to postpone the muster. And it could rain tonight.'

'I noticed the clouds building up.' She glanced a little nervously out of the window. 'But rain has to be a good thing for the paddocks, surely?'

He shrugged. 'We've had a good season, now I need a bit of dry weather to get this mob in, but what will be will be. Looking forward to seeing your mum and dad, Brett?'

Brett was with them, having declared himself not tired at all—he was too excited because his mum and dad were reunited and would be returning shortly.

And as she busied herself serving the chicken, a potato pie and green beans she listened to Brett telling Steve there was only one cloud on his horizon—how was he going to bear being parted from Rich?

'Well,' Steve said, 'I would say you're old enough to have a dog of your own. Mind you, until that happens, you can always come over and play with Rich.'

'A dog of my own,' Brett mused. 'But how would I know he'd be as much fun as Rich?'

'Most dogs are pretty good if they're brought up properly. Isn't that so, Chattie?'

'Uh—yes,' she answered with a touch of caution. 'I did take Rich to training classes, though.'

Brett sat up excitedly. 'So you know how to do it? That means you could show me!'

'Well, I won't be here long enough for that,' she said, but added as the boy's face fell, 'I'm sure your dad or Steve could help. Does your mum—like dogs?'

'She doesn't like cleaning up after them,' Brett said. 'She reckons it always falls to the mum to have to do that kind of thing.'

'I see.' Steve thought for a bit. 'Well, maybe I could housetrain it first, then hand it over, but these things don't happen overnight, old son. First we have to find a suitable puppy.'

But Brett had stars in his eyes and after dinner the only way they could get him to bed was to play several games of dominoes with him.

'I just hope we haven't put ourselves beyond the pale with Harriet over a puppy,' Chattie said ruefully when she finally got him settled for the night.

Steve glanced at her humorously. 'So do I. We'll just have to present a united front.'

Chattie started to make some coffee at the same time as she examined the strange feeling of being united in humour and a co-conspirator with Steve Kinane. But before she could diagnose the feeling thoroughly, a clap of thunder tore the air, the lights went out and she dropped the coffee-pot.

Fortunately there was nothing in it but as a flash of brilliant lightning illuminated the kitchen briefly she clung to the kitchen counter.

'Chattie?' Steve stood up. 'Are you all right?'

Her voice wouldn't work at first, then it came out sounding strained and unnatural. 'Fine, thanks.'

'Like hell,' he said, and groped his way over to her. 'Are you scared of thunder and lightning?' he asked with a tinge of incredulity.

'That…' she swallowed '…was quite some thunder and lightning.' She flinched as another crack came.

'Well, well, I wouldn't have guessed it,' he said and put his arms around her waist.

She shivered against him as he pulled her closer. 'G-guessed what?'

'That the iron maiden had any cracks—this will pass over in about ten minutes and I doubt there'll be much rain,' he added before she could take issue with the 'iron maiden' crack. 'How long it will take for the electricity to come back on is anyone's guess. I'll get some hurricane lamps going.'

Chattie closed her eyes and felt a dew of sweat break out on her brow and down her spine as more lightning flashed. 'Would you mind,' she said with difficulty, 'not moving an inch just for the moment?'

And as a peal of thunder cracked right above them, she found herself clinging to Steve Kinane as if she'd never let him go.

'Chattie,' he said into her hair, 'I promise you you're quite safe. This old house has survived many a storm and we do have a lightning conductor.'

Chattie made a supreme effort but it wasn't enough, her knees felt like jelly and her heart was pounding. 'I'm sorry to be so stupid but my intellect and my…insides just won't co-ordinate over this.' She flinched as the storm continued to provide visual and audible pyrotechnics.

'OK.' He patted her back. 'Hang on, then, we'll ride it out together.'

'What about Brett?'

'He's not scared of storms even if it does wake him. What about Rich?'

'He's shut in my bedroom—he'll be under the bed by now. He's almost as much of a ninny as I am.'

Steve laughed. 'You make a good pair. Look, it's already starting to move away.'

Chattie listened and he was right. It had started to rain but the thunder and lightning were not as close. She sighed with relief, then tensed as another loud clap of thunder came.

'There could be a few last hurrahs before it goes away completely,' Steve said comfortably, 'but never mind, this is rather pleasant.'

She blinked up at him in the gloom. 'What?'

'An armful of Chattie Winslow,' he said gravely. 'Would you not agree?'

Her lips parted and her eyes widened. 'I... I...'

'Hadn't thought about it in that light?' He lifted a wry eyebrow at her.

'No! No, I hadn't,' she added, but less certainly because, now she did come to think of it, it was very pleasant. He felt like a strong, safe haven but it was more than that. Not only did she feel safe and secure, she felt her senses stirring as a delicious awareness of her contours against the strength of his tall body overcame her.

'Maybe you should?' he suggested. 'In general, I'm a much better bet than my brother. For one thing, I'm on the spot, so to speak.'

Chattie wrenched her mind from the sensations

starting to course through her—the sensitivity of her breasts, the tremor within that the feel of his hand on her hip created—and she tried to pull away, thunder or no thunder, but he wouldn't let her go.

'Not only do you feel very pleasant, but you're a good height for me,' he said musingly. 'Short girls can be tough on one's neck.'

Chattie gasped. 'How can you? I don't believe you're...saying these things!'

'Why not?' he asked lazily. 'We could hardly be closer.'

'If you think I was faking a fear of thunder and lightning,' she said through her teeth, 'if you think that wasn't just about the worst example of it I've ever experienced, you're mistaken. You...you have to be incredibly arrogant, not to mention even more of a typical man than I gave you credit for!'

He grinned. 'All charges accepted, ma'am. Well, one thing I do know, the very womanly way you feel in my arms at the moment has me feeling all man, arrogant or otherwise.'

Damn you, she thought, it's all too true. Her mind might take issue with it but her body was loving it, arrogant or whatever.

'You're taking advantage of me, Steve Kinane,' she accused.

'Mmm,' he agreed, but as the lights came on she could see that he looked entirely unrepentant.

'What happened to our purely business proposition?'

'Flew out the window. It's also occurred to me that since Rich is hiding under a bed I might as well make hay while the sun shines—terrible metaphor in the circumstances, but you know what I mean.'

'I know exactly what you mean but that makes it even worse!'

'Well, now,' he drawled, 'what makes it really *interesting* is that you should have felt so safe in my arms, Chattie. I doubt a man who was wholly repugnant to you would have had the same effect.'

She coloured delicately, she just couldn't help herself, but her eyes were defiant. 'I may have felt safe but I still haven't forgotten the quip about stealing the silver, however it was made.'

He looked down at her thoughtfully. 'And I'm still not sure what your intentions are, Miss Winslow, but it doesn't alter the fact that it's impossible for us to be like this and be physically unaffected.'

'If you would let me go—' she tried to keep her voice steady '—you would find that you're quite safe from…my intentions.'

He smiled fleetingly. 'Problem is, I don't want to be safe from you—not like this, anyway.'

They stared into each other's eyes. And Chattie discovered that, deep inside her, she didn't want to be safe from this man. There was something about him that attracted her, something elementary and strangely powerful, but it was accompanied by so much she couldn't rationalize, she'd be a fool to let herself be carried away…

'There's a little pulse at the base of your throat beating like a tom-tom,' he said softly, and put his fingertip lightly on it.

She bit her lip.

'And your mouth was made for kissing,' he added

barely audibly as that straying finger outlined her lips. 'Why don't we give it a test run?'

For the life of her, she couldn't control the quiver of her lips any more than she could block from her senses the sheer impact of Steve Kinane's body on hers. Hard and muscled, the impact was little short of electrifying.

'Let's not,' she said huskily as she tried desperately to gather her defences. 'This is ridiculous.'

'On the contrary, this is a force between a man and a woman who are attracted to each other—and it can happen with nothing so pale and wishy-washy as ''liking'' involved at all,' he said dryly.

'No,' she disagreed unevenly. 'This is your way of showing the contempt you really feel for me. For instance, I'd like to bet my bottom dollar that once you've kissed me you will make some cutting reference to me and your brother.'

Something glinted briefly in his eyes but she couldn't identify it. 'OK.' He shrugged. 'You be the judge—of whether you even remember my brother afterwards.'

'Steve,' she said urgently, 'no!'

'Chattie, yes. You can always lay the blame on the storm if you like, I probably will. Or—' his dark eyes glinted with something she could readily identify this time: wicked satire '—you could stick to the ''typical man'' bit but, whatever, I'm stuck on a course I can't get off.'

If you dare respond to this, Charlotte Winslow, I'll never speak to you again! she warned herself.

Only to have him read her mind—probably from the stubborn set of her lips. So he didn't bother with them. He cradled her hips to him. She had on the three-quarter-length skirt and white blouse she'd worn the night before, but the thin floral cotton and a pair of bikini briefs were little protection against the feel of his hands on her bottom and she started to breathe raggedly. He raised a wry eyebrow.

Then he slid his hands up to around her waist. 'I can nearly span this,' he said softly. 'Let me guess, twenty—twenty-one inches?'

'That's my business,' she said huskily.

'Well, I would…' those tantalizing hands moved upwards to her ribcage '…estimate thirty-two, twenty-one, thirty-two.'

'From your considerable experience of women, no doubt!' Her eyes flashed.

'Some,' he agreed.

'Then let me tell you, I despise men who go about mentally measuring busts, waists and hips!'

He smiled faintly. 'You're right, it's rather adolescent and not a common occupation of mine—must be something about the perfection of your figure that got to me.' He shrugged. 'Mind you, it doesn't help when you swing them.' His hands descended again to her hips.

'I don't, deliberately,' she denied. 'I just—walk.'

'Then it comes naturally? I'm glad,' he murmured. 'But it's still a bit of a trial. Then there's your skin. Another trial.' This time he slid his hands up her arms. 'Like silk,' he commented. He circled his arms around her again. 'And you're so fair, it comes as a bit of a shock to discover all this delicate beauty has a mind like a steel trap.'

'You better believe it,' she warned, but it was getting harder and harder to maintain her hostility for the fact of the matter was that she was in a trap, a silken trap, she thought bitterly, but one of her own making?

She had always been scared of thunder and lightning—it was the one area where Bridget was the stronger of the two of them. Bridget loved storms provided she was safe from the destructive effects of them. She even seemed to gather a kind of kinetic energy from them. But how foolish had she, Chattie, been to reveal this weakness of hers to this man in this way?

In other words, could she absolve him of some of the blame because she'd brought about the situation unthinkingly? And was as vulnerable to it as he was, if she was painfully honest?

'Miss Winslow?' he said very quietly.

She swallowed. Nestled in his arms like this she could breathe in the pure man aroma of him as well as the freshly laundered tang of the bush shirt and clean jeans he'd changed into. She could see the blue shadows on his jaw and the lines beside his mouth— and the question in his eyes.

A little sob of pure frustration escaped her and she raised her hands to cup his face, then stood on her toes and kissed him lightly on the mouth. And said against his lips, 'This may be my fault but it's still insanity and it changes nothing. Will you let me go now, please?'

'In a moment. I'm never one for leaving a task half finished.'

And he pulled her right into him, teased her lips apart and started to kiss her properly.

When he'd finished, she was quivering with desire,

surrounded sensually by his strength and masculinity and completely focused on Steve Kinane—her enemy.

'So,' he said to her dazed look as he let her go, 'what was so insane about that?'

She stared into his dark, saturnine eyes and did the only thing left for her to do—she swung on her heel and retreated to her bedroom.

Rich came out from under the bed to greet her eagerly and she patted him briefly, then leant back against the door to steady her breathing and take stock. But a more bizarre scenario she couldn't envisage.

To fall for a man who was going to hate her by association if nothing else once he learnt the truth was—asking for trouble, she thought shakily. And why wouldn't he put her in the same basket as Bridget? She was the one conniving to get Mark Kinane back to Bridget. Or, at least admit his responsibility towards her sister's unborn child.

Nor could Steve have made his sentiments clearer towards Mark being trapped into marriage.

She straightened and went to sit on the bed with a sigh.

'Tell him the truth now, Rich?' she said wearily. 'Before this gets totally out of hand? I think I'm going to have to. I don't know why I just didn't do it in the first place.'

She closed her eyes and mentally pictured Bridget at home and getting more and more disturbed as the days went by—and who knew how many more days would go by until Mark Kinane touched his home base?

Not only that but how many more days to endure in the company of a man who was diabolically attractive to you but didn't trust you and could only end up despising you?

'No, it's madness,' she said to Rich, and stood up. 'I'll tell him right now.'

She was halfway to the door when she heard a motor start up. Not Merlene's bike with its distinctive roar but the ute Steve drove around the property.

'Damn,' she muttered. 'Where's he going at this time of night?'

Wherever it was, two hours later he still hadn't returned and Chattie gave up and went to bed, but determined to have things out with Steve Kinane first thing in the morning.

Like many good intentions, it didn't happen that way.

CHAPTER FIVE

AT STEVE'S request, Merlene joined them at breakfast the next morning before Chattie got a chance to get him on his own. So that, when she did encounter him for the first time that morning, it was not only in Merlene's company, but Brett was labouring through his porridge as well.

Beyond exchanging cool glances, she and the boss of Mount Helena did not address each other but that cool, dark glance from Steve Kinane sent a shiver down her spine.

'Looks like a council of war,' Merlene commented as Chattie dished up steak and eggs.

'You could say so,' he said to Merlene. 'We've got a house party coming up in a few days. Five people, two couples—thank you—' Steve said to Chattie as she put his plate in front of him '—and a single. They'll be here for two nights, Tuesday and Wednesday, arriving late Tuesday afternoon and leaving on Thursday morning after breakfast. On Wednesday I'd like a formal dinner party for ten. The other four people will be Harriet and Jack and the shire chairman and his wife.'

'Uh-oh, it is a council of war!' Merlene buttered her toast. 'State of the roads, a drought relief fund for when the next one hits, noxious weed control?'

'Yes,' he agreed.

'And designed to bring home to the pompous old

git of a chairman the fact that he could get booted out at the next council election—good on yer!'

Steve grimaced. 'In a civilized manner but basically—yes.'

''Bout time you ran yourself,' Merlene commented. 'Your dad did an excellent job.'

'We'll see,' Steve said briefly. 'But Chattie is going to need some more of your time, Merlene,' he added.

Chattie opened her mouth to say that she wouldn't be available for the house party but Merlene spoke immediately.

'It's no good asking me to wait tables or cook. I'm all thumbs at that kind of thing. But I guess I could make an exception and do dishes and help with the cleaning and tidying up.'

'Thank you,' Steve said gravely. 'I'm sure Chattie would really appreciate it.'

'Uh—yes, but—'

Brett interrupted. 'Chattie, can I come and see Rich every day when Mum and Dad get home?'

'Uh—yes, but—'

It was Steve who interrupted this time. 'That's the second time you've sounded less than positive,' he said to her. 'Come into the office for a moment, please.' He got up.

Chattie took a very deep breath, and followed him.

He sat down at the desk but didn't invite her to sit in the only other chair. He swivelled his chair sideways so he could watch her and said coldly, 'You're about to do a bunk, aren't you?'

'It would hardly be a bunk, since I have no real reason to be here, as you've pointed out several times,' she commented.

'I would have thought you now had an excellent reason to stay on.' And he raked her from head to toe with a glance that was both insolent and contemptuous. 'Going to pretend it didn't happen, Chattie?'

She coloured but her eyes were steady. 'What happened was due to—an involuntary but all the same—thoughtlessness on my part and—'

'Like hell,' he shot back. 'Listen, if you feel you need some kind of a release from Mark to take up with his brother, you don't. He is obviously finished with you, Miss Winslow. Do you honestly think he'd be driving halfway round the country otherwise?'

'Look,' she began, 'things aren't quite what they seem—'

'Do you think I don't know that?' he broke in roughly. 'So tell me why you came and why you're about to scuttle away. Does Mark know something about you that mightn't appeal to me? Something that could be—awkward for you were it to be revealed later? I'm thinking along the lines of a history of promiscuity, perhaps?'

Chattie went white and immediately made a decision that was quite contrary to the decision she had made the night before. 'You misunderstand me, Mr Kinane,' she said icily. 'I was theorizing when I said that it would hardly be a bunk if I were to leave. In fact, I have no intention of leaving you in the lurch, not for the time being anyway, so you may relax.'

He sat up and frowned at her. 'What about the things that aren't quite what they "seem"?'

She shrugged. 'Another mistaken impression of yours. I was not asking to be kissed last night. I have no intention of allowing it to happen again and I wouldn't put it to the test if I were you otherwise you will find yourself even more short-staffed than you already are.'

His gaze narrowed and he rubbed his jaw. 'So why *were* you so bloody hesitant in the kitchen?'

Chattie thought swiftly. 'There are some things I need to know about this house party. It's all very well to dump numbers in my lap but I need more than that.'

'Like what?' He eyed her suspiciously.

Perhaps it helps to have a mind like a steel trap, she reflected as she pulled out a chair and sat down at the desk, assuming an earnest expression. 'Could you tell me a bit about these guests, please? It helps if you know who you're catering for.'

'On your present record, Chattie, which in my estimation is that you cook like an angel,' he said dryly, 'just keep on the way you've been going.'

She looked genuinely frustrated. 'But are they young, old, middle-aged or what?'

'What difference does it make?'

'In my experience, unless you're of Italian origin, for example, pasta and pizza are young to middle-aged dishes. The same goes for Thai, Chinese and Indian cuisine—it doesn't do much for older people who've been reared on roast beef unless they've done a stint in the Middle to Far East. Salads can be another touchy generational issue. A lot of older people would far rather have vegetables.'

'I see. You obviously take these things very seriously.' He looked amused for the first time.

'I do.' This was quite true too. 'So, although I can be a very traditional cook, it would be nice to know if I didn't have to stick to roast beef and three veg,' she said.

He grimaced. 'They're a mixed bag, I'm afraid. One couple—he's the local vet—are in their middle thirties. The second couple—they run the neighbouring property—are fiftyish but quite "with it". So are Harriet and Jack. The shire chairman and his lady, however—' he tilted his chair back and looked amused '—would definitely fit into the "roast beef, three veg" clan.'

Chattie wrinkled her brow. 'OK, so apart from the formal dinner, I can be a little adventurous, by the sound of it. What about the single? And you yourself?'

'I'm easy. The single? She's in her mid-twenties and very "with it". She's a journalist and she's doing a piece on the station.'

'Uh-huh!' She sat up, thoroughly on her mettle now. 'Would you like me to prepare a list of menus for your consideration?'

He laughed softly. 'No, thank you. Since there is no lady of the house, consider yourself the ultimate authority—just don't kill yourself in the process, Chattie,' he warned. 'We're not trying to be a five-star hotel.'

'All I'll be doing is making sure they're comfortable and well fed.' She got up. 'Oh, one other thing. I seem to be in the best guest bedroom—shall I move out?'

'No,' he said slowly. 'We've got plenty of bedrooms. Stay put.'

'Thank you. Well—' she got up '—back to the mill.'

They exchanged glances. Then she added softly but intently, 'I meant it.'

'Yes, miss,' he responded. 'Are you the terror teacher of your TAFE College?'

'No, but you'd be wise to take me seriously, Steve Kinane.'

'Oh, I do, Chattie. Well, until this blasted house party is over you've got me on a good behaviour bond so to speak.' He looked torn between supreme irritation and some wryly self-directed humour.

'Thank you,' she said gravely, and departed.

But Steve Kinane stared at the wall for some moments after she'd left and asked himself a few pointed questions. Why had he not sent this intriguing, mysterious, infuriating girl packing at the first opportunity despite being left in the lurch with Brett and no Slim? What was she hiding? How was he going to cope with living in the same house with her and not laying a finger on her?

'Bridget,' Chattie said into her phone, later in the day, 'as I explained, the problem is that no one knows where Mark is at the moment. He just took off apparently. But everyone seems to think that he will get in touch with the station so a few more days may be all I need. How are you?'

'Sick as a dog,' Bridget replied, then requested a reassurance from Chattie that she hadn't revealed the truth to Steve Kinane.

Chattie bit her lip. 'Bridge, no, I haven't, but if I can't find Mark I may have to. It—well, I won't do it without consulting you, so just hang in there. Listen, you're not going to believe this,' she said in a bid to cheer her sister up, 'but I've got a temporary job on the station. Which is just as well because I would have outworn my welcome well and truly by now otherwise!'

Several minutes later she ended the call feeling somewhat reassured that the rather comical account she'd given of being the temporary housekeeper at Mount Helena had cheered Bridget up.

The next couple of days were extraordinarily busy, but all the appearances of a truce between herself and Steve Kinane existed.

She wasn't sure how she did it—then it occurred to her he must have contributed—but she concentrated on being as natural as she could in his company. Deep thought had convinced her it was the only way to go, since she'd made the—insane? Angry certainly—decision to stay on. Being busy and doing the things she loved had to have helped, of course. And it was a particularly satisfying house to be in charge of.

Still, it was strange, she acknowledged, that they could be in such discord on one level yet, outwardly, almost 'matey' so that her natural liveliness, very much on the back burner until now, began to reappear. But he did provide her with one break that turned out to be a real treat, although it also provided a true test of their truce.

She and Brett got a tour of the property by helicopter and her enthusiasm for the flight, piloted by Steve, was almost as great as the little boy's—Brett's greatest ambition was to become a helicopter pilot.

It was a Sunday, the day before Jack and Harriet were due back, and Chattie had been asked to pack a picnic and bring along swimming costumes for herself and Brett.

'It's so big,' she said to Steve in wonderment as Mount Helena unfolded below her. They were wearing headphones and mikes so they could talk over the noise. 'Do you know every inch of it—is it possible?'

'Well, not every inch, but I've been flying over it since I was eighteen,' he replied.

'Do you muster by helicopter?' she asked as she spied a mob of cattle on the move towards a thread of green winding across the plain, indicating, she guessed, a water course.

'Sometimes. Over the really rough country it's easier but we also use motor bikes and ringers on horses or a combination of the three.'

'I would love to see a muster,' she said wistfully.

'If you're here long enough you will. OK—' he pointed through the wind screen '—see that big patch of green? It's a billabong and it has to be a pretty serious drought for it to dry up. We'll have lunch there.'

So they landed and spent a lovely couple of hours exploring the billabong, revelling in the shade of the gum-trees that lined it and splashing in the shallows.

'This is a very unique experience,' Chattie said as she set out her lunch on a rug. 'Let's see, egg and lettuce sandwiches, ham and tomato, Vegemite, which I happen to know goes down well with young Mr Barlow but you don't have to partake of them.' She glinted a dancing look at Steve. 'Uh—and some cold chicken. Do help yourselves. There are lamingtons and tea to follow.'

She'd slipped a white T-shirt over her swimming costume and she sat down cross-legged on the rug.

Steve and Brett wore only their swim wear, in

Steve's case dark green board shorts. He'd helped Brett construct an elementary raft with branches and some rope from the helicopter, and Brett was lying tummy down on it, scanning the depths of the billabong as he paddled it with his hands.

'Leave him,' Chattie said as Steve was about to call him to lunch. 'He'll come when he's hungry.'

'Tell me what's so unique about this?' he invited as he helped himself to a drumstick and several sandwiches.

'Well, I've got this picture in my mind of the map of Australia spread out all around us, and just the three of us on it.' She wrinkled her brow. 'Maybe some cattle as well, but that's all.'

'Funny you should say that,' he said slowly. 'I sometimes get the same feeling.'

'Do you enjoy the feeling?'

'I do enjoy the sensation of space, I sometimes revel in solitude, not that this is precisely solitude.'

She shaded her eyes with her hand and watched the way the sunlight filtered through the leaves above was dancing on the water. 'So do I.'

He glanced narrowly at her. 'Didn't you tell me you had a sister?'

Chattie tensed inwardly. 'Yes.'

'Do you live with her?'

'Yes. We're pretty close, actually, but this is different,' she said slowly.

He studied her thoughtfully, and suddenly realized he was on the receiving end of a similar, rather absorbed contemplation.

'What?' he queried, looking comically alarmed.

A faint blush stained her cheeks because she'd

found herself musing on the subject of just how much of a true loner he was; and how much the memory of the kiss they'd shared had occupied her mind ever since it had happened.

Of course, they had to be related topics, she realized. Nor was she in any way helped to forget that second topic as he lounged back in his board shorts on the rug.

If it weren't for Brett, I could happily do it again.

The thought raced through her mind and made her quite dizzy but a relaxed, slightly damp Steve Kinane, tanned, muscular and beautifully proportioned, was almost too much to bear. Then there was the desire she identified as a growing longing to get to know him better…

Be still, my crazy heart, she told herself, then leapt to her feet with a cry of pain as what felt like a very fine but red-hot skewer pierced the tender flesh under her arm. 'Ouch!' She swatted at the area frantically then felt another sting.

Steve was on his feet in a second and he picked her up with his hands about her waist and jumped into the billabong with her.

'What…why?' she gasped and swallowed some water.

'Green ants. They bite like the devil. Here. You can stand.'

She found her feet and he wrestled her T-shirt off, then unceremoniously pulled the straps of her swimming costume down, exposing her breasts.

'No…don't,' she spluttered. 'What are you doing?'

'No choice,' he said laconically and pushed her below the water to the level of her chin.

The relief was blessed. 'Holy smoke,' she said, forgetting her nakedness for the moment, 'that hurt!'

'They do,' he agreed. 'The longer you stay like that, the better.'

'He's right,' Brett called.

'That's all very well,' Chattie remarked, folding her arms over her chest, 'but they must be drowned by now and modesty prevents me from—'

'They would be drowned by now but the cold water will help soothe the sting and modesty is—well, you're quite safe from me if that's worrying you,' Steve said gravely.

She shot him a look. 'I should hope so.'

'Not,' he responded with an entirely wicked glint in his eyes, 'that it's easy to be unmoved by such sheer feminine perfection, but I am on a good-behaviour bond.'

Chattie's hair was dripping into her eyes and she raised her hands to smooth the water out of it.

'Even harder if you do that,' he added barely audibly.

She clamped her arms around herself speedily. 'Will you go away?' she requested *sotto voce*, but with her grey eyes growing stormy. 'You were the one who…got me like this.'

'Only in your best interests.' He looked quite serious but she knew he was laughing at her.

'Well, they've been well and truly served now!'

'Maybe.' He grimaced. 'Mine, however, are another matter. Still—' he shrugged '—I'm told cold water helps there too.'

Chattie took a breath as their gazes locked.

His dark hair was plastered to his head and his eyelashes clumped together—but he was breathtakingly attractive with his broad, wet shoulders and his white teeth. And for a moment it was impossible not to imagine them alone in the billabong. Alone, and matching her paler skin to his strong, tanned body, her curves to his lines and angles as the cool water swirled over and around them.

She closed her eyes for a long, sensuous moment and when she opened them it was to find that all humour, wicked or otherwise, had gone from his expression. She tensed. But he looked away first, then turned away and climbed out, calling to Brett at the same time, and things got back to normal.

Well, almost normal, she was to think later that evening. Nothing more had been said but there'd been one occasion when they'd been caught in a little world of their own again, she and Steve. When he'd helped her climb out of the helicopter his hand had lingered on her elbow.

It was the lightest pressure but she'd paused as her whole body had been invaded by an awareness of him and a strange but lovely sensation at the pit of her stomach had made her feel as if the world had tripped...

She'd stared into his eye with her heart starting to beat heavily but Brett had intervened, by jumping down beside her, and Steve had released her without a word—and the world had righted itself.

'You seem to know quite a few tricks of the trade,' Merlene said the next morning when they were dusting and polishing guest bedrooms and making up beds.

Chattie explained about her domestic-science training then straightened from the perfectly made bed with her hands on her hips. 'These guest bedrooms are kind of bare. No ornaments, no vases or that kind of thing.'

'Kid, when you got a house with six bedrooms excluding the annexe, and five bathrooms, it takes a powerful lot of work to keep it all dusted and clean. So Slim keeps one guest bedroom up to date, yours, and only breaks out the others when necessary, which ain't often.'

'Breaks out?' Chattie wrinkled her brow.

'There's a store room next to the linen press you may not have come across. It's full of knick-knacks and things.'

'Can I have a look?' Chattie asked with a tremor of excitement.

Merlene shrugged. 'Maybe Steve woulda mentioned it if he'd wanted—'

'He did say to consider myself the ultimate authority, well, below you, of course,' she hastened to assure Merlene quite untruthfully but most diplomatically.

'OK! I must say it all used to look lovely when his mum was alive and of course when—'

But she stopped as they heard a vehicle drive up to the garden gate. 'Who would that be?'

Brett solved the mystery by dashing past, yelling, 'Mum, Dad, guess what? You just have to buy me my very own dog or else I'll come and live with Steve and Chattie permam-m-m-ently!'

Merlene looked heavenwards. 'Her ladyship has returned. You watch yourself with her—she can be a right bitch.'

But Harriet Barlow had a glow about her of a woman deeply in love. She wafted into the house on the arm of a lean, freckled, fair-haired man and they shared an affectionate reunion with Brett, got introduced to Rich then became aware of Chattie—Merlene had retreated to the kitchen.

'You must be the godsend Steve mentioned—I'm Jack Barlow.' Brett's father extended his hand to Chattie. 'Thanks so much for looking after this young tyke!'

'It was my pleasure, but actually it was Rich who did most of it,' Chattie responded with a grin.

'Anyway, thanks,' Harriet remarked. 'I must say I got the impression the other night that you were just passing through but I may have been mistaken.'

'I was until Slim collapsed,' Chattie explained, then decided to get it over and done with. 'Actually I came up to see Mark but—we had a few crossed wires, I guess you could say.'

Harriet raised her eyebrows but that was all and they gathered Brett and his belongings and left.

'Tra-la, tra-la!' Merlene re-emerged. 'Until the next time.'

Chattie laughed. 'OK, lead me on to Aladdin's cave.'

The store room did turn out to be a bit like Aladdin's cave and Chattie had a marvellous time with all the neatly stored items she found: pretty scatter cushions for the armchairs, thick, thirsty monogrammed towels in jewel-bright colours, vases, ornaments and so on.

'That looks so much better,' she said to herself as she wandered through each bedroom on the afternoon the guests were due to arrive.

She'd consulted with the hand who looked after the

house garden and, although there weren't a lot of flowers to be had, there were some interesting shrubs with variegated or coloured leaves, tiny star-like blossoms and gum tips that filled the air with either a lemony or honey fragrance that she'd been allowed to plunder. She'd made up arrangements for each room and several for the lounge and dining room.

She was also confident she had everything else under control, and she'd taken an initiative. In a corner of the dining room she'd set up a trolley with a coffee machine she'd found, cups, milk, sugar, home-made biscuits in a barrel and a kettle for those who preferred tea.

She was studying it while trying to do up her fine gold chain necklace she always wore when Steve came up soundlessly behind her. 'Good thinking,' he pronounced. 'They can help themselves.'

She jumped.

'Sorry, didn't mean to startle you, Miss Winslow,' he said with a smile growing at the back of his eyes, 'but I must say you look the part. Can I help with that?'

Chattie looked down at herself, then at the necklace in her hand. She wore a chic slim corn-coloured three-quarter-length linen skirt and a sleeveless navy-blue top. Her hair was tied back with a colourful yellow and navy scarf and strappy low sandals completed her outfit.

'The part?'

'You look,' he paused, 'like the lady of the house.'

Colour rushed into her cheeks. 'I...only intend to be the housekeeper and to stay in the background as much as possible. Am I too—dressy?' she asked with concern.

He shook his head, took the chain from her and stepped round her to deal with the clasp. 'You're always dressy,' he said with his fingers lingering on the back of her neck, and causing the fine hairs to stand up all over her body. Then he went on his way—leaving Chattie electrified but frowning in confusion as she watched him go.

An hour later the first guests, from the neighbouring property, flew in followed closely by the vet and his wife, who brought the journalist with them.

'It's on for old and young,' Merlene said humorously. 'That woman, the journo, has been here before poking around and gathering info for some kind of book or article, but I wouldn't be surprised if she's got her eye on Steve and all the rest is humbug.'

Chattie looked up from the canapés she was preparing, to be served with sundowners on the veranda. 'Really?'

The 'journo' was a slim, elegant brunette with lavender-blue eyes and had been introduced to Chattie as Sasha Kelly. She'd contrived to be slim and elegant despite being all kitted out in khaki and wearing short boots, and, beyond the definite surprise in her lovely eyes on being presented to the housekeeper, she'd been rather nice.

They all had, Ray and Lucy Cook, the vet and his wife, and John and Joan Jackson, the triple Js as they called themselves, from the station next door—a hundred miles away.

Chattie had shown them all to their rooms, assured

them if they needed anything they only had to ask, and retired immediately to the kitchen.

She scooped some caviare onto the circle of hard-boiled egg atop a round biscuit, and paused for thought.

'It's a bit surprising he's not already married, isn't it?'

Merlene wiped her hands on her apron. 'Oh, he—'
She stopped as Steve came into the kitchen.

Chattie's eyes widened. He'd already surprised her twice today. Once, when he'd come upon her admiring the coffee trolley and again when, for the first time, she'd seen him out of jeans and a bush shirt and look-ing rather different but just as impressive, if not more so, in bone moleskins and a cream-and-red-checked shirt.

This time, though, it was his eyes that surprised her. They were hard and cool as he surveyed the scene in the kitchen and made her wonder nervously what she and Merlene had done wrong.

And a beat passed before he said with no particular inflection, also nerve-racking, 'I'm about to serve drinks and we should be ready for dinner in an hour.'

'Oh.' Chattie licked caviar from her fingertip and started to spoon it more rapidly. 'There, all done.' She indicated the two silver platters laden with artistic and delicious-looking bite-sized eats. 'Will I bring them through?'

'No, thanks.' He picked up the two platters and walked out.

Chattie turned to Merlene. 'What's gone wrong?'

Merlene merely shrugged, although Chattie did notice that she looked oddly embarrassed. But, from then on, Chattie was far too busy to give it further thought.

By ten-thirty the house was quiet, the last dish had been put away, the breakfast table laid and Chattie was able to retire to her bedroom with a cup of tea, which she took out to the veranda. Rich woke up and came to sit at her feet.

'Well,' she murmured to him, 'the entrée went down well. The main course of lamb and noodles with plum sauce and sesame seeds was much applauded and so was the apricot and sour cream slice.'

Rich yawned.

'Sorry—am I keeping you up? I was even,' Chattie continued, 'asked for my recipes, although I must confess Ms Sasha Kelly, who I first thought was quite nice, was the only one who did not appear to be impressed.'

She looked thoughtful for a moment, then shrugged. 'I think Merlene's right—Sasha may have her sights on Steve. The other thing is—the boss is not in a good mood. I can just *feel* it.'

This time Rich stiffened, growled, then leapt at the wire screen as a furry creature slipped down the outside of it from the veranda roof into the bushes. In the process Chattie upset her tea down her blouse and it was still hot enough to cause her to yelp in pain.

At the same time Steve Kinane loomed up out of the darkness.

'What are you doing here?' Chattie gasped, getting up and holding her top away from her skin. 'Sit, Rich,' she commanded.

'I usually take a stroll in the garden before I turn

in,' he replied, 'so I heard the kerfuffle—it was only a possum. No need to get your knickers in a twist.'

'I know it was only a possum! I'm not completely "citified",' she answered with some chagrin. 'Rich made me spill my tea, that's all.'

'Are you burnt? Let me see.' Without waiting for an answer, he pulled her top up and scanned her skin above the waistband of her skirt, and her breasts cupped in a navy bra trimmed with ivory and pink lace. His eyebrows rose but all he said was, 'Your skin's a bit pink. Go and splash yourself with cool water and I'll get us a drink.'

He let the top fall and walked away through her bedroom.

Chattie blinked several times, then shook her head bewilderedly and took herself to her bathroom.

When she reappeared on the veranda she had her pyjamas on beneath a yellow terry-towelling robe.

Steve was waiting for her with two glasses of brandy.

'Better?' he queried.

'Yes. I'll be fine.' She sat down. 'I don't even think I'm injured enough to deserve a brandy,' she added ruefully.

'Have it all the same,' he recommended. 'It's been quite a night for you, I would imagine.'

'I think it all went well, although at one stage Merlene got quite panic-stricken, which I didn't expect!' She laughed.

He grinned. 'It went exceptionally well. I'd like to pay my respects.'

Chattie's eyes widened. 'I thought you were upset with me.'

He lifted his dark eyes to her. 'No.'

'Well, about something, then.'

He paused. 'How could you tell?'

'I don't know, I just could,' she said slowly.

'Something came up, that's all. It's now—sorted.'

'Why do I get the feeling it isn't?' she said, barely audibly.

'Chattie, I know you have your finger on the pulse of this house as any good housekeeper would, but everything is OK. The guests are most impressed. So am I.'

Part of her harboured a little question mark still, but she had no choice but to allow it to rest.

'Thank you. So. You're all going out and about tomorrow?'

'Yes, we'll be out of your hair apart from breakfast, lunch and dinner.'

'What will you be doing?' she asked curiously.

'I've implemented a few changes recently, mainly to do with paddock and weed management. Often, when you do that, you hold an open day for the district, generally in conjunction with the manufacturers of a new piece of machinery, equipment or product of some kind. This is a test run for a proper open day.'

'Oh, that's interesting.' She looked into the dark night as if she was picturing Mount Helena in a new and rather fascinating way, then something struck her. 'Does it…' she hesitated '…also have to do with promoting oneself for election to the shire council?'

'No flies on you, Miss Winslow. Yes.'

She wrinkled her brow. 'May I make a comment?'

'Be my guest,' he said wryly.

'Only if you promise not to take offence.'

'I'll see.' He looked amused.

She took a breath. 'You seem to live and breathe Mount Helena and this "cattle" life.'

'You don't approve?'

She gestured. 'It's not that at all, I'm coming to think it's rather lovely, but...' she hesitated again '...I'm wondering how much of a loner you have to be to really stick to it.'

He grimaced. 'To do it properly does take a hell of a lot of time, but I'm not entirely uncultured, if that's what you're implying.'

'No, I wasn't!'

'Tell the truth, Chattie. Compared to such a multi-talented person as yourself, do you perceive me as a philistine?' He drained his brandy. 'Or perhaps you're comparing me to Mark?'

Her lips parted in surprise.

'Who is quite cultured but no good at running a cattle station.' He stood up.

She followed suit. 'I believe I've been misunder-stood. I—'

'No you haven't, Chattie. Goodnight,' he said abruptly and left via the garden.

She stared after him, then sat down again with a frown and the helpless feeling that she'd unwittingly brought back Steve Kinane's dark mood despite being no wiser as to its origin.

After the success of the evening it was a lowering and troubling thought.

CHAPTER SIX

THINGS began to go wrong almost from the start of the next day.

Chattie overslept and had an almighty rush to get breakfast on the table in time. And John Jackson sought her out to tell her that his wife, Joan, had a migraine and would be staying in bed.

'Oh, I'm sorry. I'll keep an eye on her, Mr Jackson,' she promised. 'Is there anything special you'd like me to do?'

'No, thanks, Miss Winslow. Dark, rest and quiet are what she needs, although, perhaps a small meal when it's over?'

'My pleasure,' Chattie murmured, suddenly conscious of Steve's dark gaze on her.

She had ignored him other than a formal greeting when she'd first encountered him at the breakfast table, not hard to do as she'd juggled a full breakfast for six people without giving off the vibes that she was in a rush.

But somehow she'd got through it all and the party was now leaving the table to get ready for their morning in the paddocks. As their gazes clashed, though, she got the feeling that Steve Kinane had divined her less-than-top-notch performance—or was she imagining the tinge of irony in his gaze?

Then Sasha Kelly, again kitted out in khaki, although the previous evening she'd looked stunning in midnight-blue, asked Chattie if she'd mind doing some washing and ironing for her.

'I've been on the hop for nearly a week now researching articles, and I just haven't had a chance to get to it,' she said airily. 'Besides which, I'm sure you're much better at laundry than I am.'

Whether intended as a sting in the tail or not, Chattie discovered herself in the mood to take it as such.

She flicked her hair back and put a hand on her hip. 'I'd be very happy to show you the washing machine and the ironing-board, Miss Kelly. Now—' she turned regally to the rest of the party '—just in case you get hungry during the morning, I've prepared an esky with some cool drinks and snacks—perhaps you'd like to be in charge of it, Steve?'

'Certainly, Miss Winslow,' he said with mock deference—it had to be mock, Chattie decided—although the rest of the party appeared to be electrified by her brush with Sasha Kelly.

'Fine. Well, off you go.' She waved a hand. 'Have a lovely morning!' And she strode purposefully towards the kitchen.

To find Merlene doubled up with laughter.

'You learn fast, kid!' she spluttered.

'You heard? Who does she think she is?' Chattie asked incredulously.

'I heard it all. Told you.'

'I am not in a good mood now, thanks to her.'

'Wouldn't be surprised if she isn't either,' Merlene commented.

'On the other hand,' Chattie said slowly, calming

down a little, 'am I supposed to do their washing and ironing?'

'Heaven's above, no!' Merlene looked horrified. 'None of the others would have dreamt of asking you.'

Chattie mulled this over. 'So she really meant to make me look like a domestic rather than an academic? Why?'

'Some women are just built that way. Can't tolerate ''lookers'' in any shape or form. And Steve is quite a catch.'

Before Chattie got a chance to respond to this, the phone rang. It was Harriet Barlow, distraught because Brett had disappeared and had they seen him?

'No,' Chattie said down the line. 'Why would we have?'

'He wanted to come and see your blasted dog, that's why. But I said I didn't have the time to drive him over this morning, and do you realize there are two dams between our house and yours and he is strictly forbidden to leave our garden on his own?'

'Then you should have kept an eye on him,' Chattie said crisply.

'Who the hell do you think you are? It's your stupid dog that's caused all the trouble!'

'Listen, lady, don't get sassy with me, I don't work for you. Get on your bicycle and start looking for him! We'll do the same from this end!' She put the phone down and explained things tersely to Merlene.

'The only thing is,' she finished up, 'what car are we going to use to look for him?'

'We'll use my bike—it's perfect and you can double up,' Merlene suggested. 'Poor little tyke,' she added.

So Chattie climbed up behind Merlene when they

should have been cleaning up after breakfast and starting to prepare lunch. And they roared around the property on the bike while picturing Brett drowned in a dam or lost in the wilderness, until they found him asleep under a tree about halfway between his house and the main homestead.

Harriet drove up not long afterwards and, to give her credit, she appeared to have been worried out of her mind, from the loving reunion she lavished on her son. Not that Brett seemed to understand what all the fuss was about.

'Look, he's welcome to come and spend a couple of hours with us,' Chattie offered. 'He and Rich just play for hours on end.'

'Thank you,' Harriet said stiffly. Then she sighed. 'I'm sorry. When I get worried I tend to let fly. You've been wonderful with Brett and I really appreciate it.'

Chattie blinked but Harriet was obviously genuine. 'Thanks. To be honest I don't usually let fly, but someone had already ruffled my feathers a bit. Oh, my stars!' She clapped a hand to her forehead. 'I forgot all about Mrs Jackson! If she's up and about she'll have no idea what's going on!'

But Joan Jackson, when Chattie cautiously peeped into her bedroom after they got back, was fast asleep.

'I'm beginning to feel as if I'm trying to run through heavy water,' she commented to Merlene as she got back to the kitchen and saw the time.

'Care for a bit of advice?'

'Only too happy to listen!'

'Stick the lunch out on the long table on the front veranda and let them fend for themselves. And you just concentrate on your cooking. I'll fix the rest, although I'll leave the dinner table to you.'

'Merlene, you're a doll!'

Lunch came and went without incident although Steve did enquire what Brett was doing amongst them.

Chattie explained briefly.

He raised his eyebrows. 'It never rains but pours.'

'Oh, he's no trouble, but it did wreak a bit of havoc with my timetable, that's all.'

'You look a little—frazzled.'

She subjected him to an annoyed glance and announced that she would be the essence of cool, calm collectedness for the evening.

His gaze lingered on her. 'That should be well worth seeing.'

'I don't know what you mean—I often find you hard to understand, in fact, but I'd appreciate it if you'd remove yourself and all these people as you promised you would!'

'Done,' he replied promptly, but added with a gleam of sheer satire in his eyes, 'Although I must tell you, you've taken the position of housekeeper to new—er—heights.'

He walked away without a backward glance.

Chattie bit her lip, and stayed where she was, lost in thought for a minute or two.

At four o'clock, she felt much more in control of things, having taken her advice to herself along the lines of being purely professional in this job.

She showered and changed—Brett had been retrieved by his mother—and, just to reaffirm her composure, she slipped into the music room for a couple of minutes. As her fingers slid across the ivories very softly a sense of peace came to her, as it always did. Then the door clicked open behind her and she turned to see Joan Jackson.

'Oh, Mrs Jackson! I hope I didn't wake you—how are you feeling?'

'No, you didn't wake me—may I call you Chattie? I've been coming out of it for about an hour now, but when I heard the piano I thought I must be dreaming. You play beautifully, my dear!'

'Thank you!' But Chattie looked perplexed. 'Dreaming?'

'Well, wafted back to the days when my good friend Christine—Steve's mother—used to play that piano. She was very musical too. Has he told you about her?'

'No,' Chattie said.

Joan looked around. 'I think there's a picture of her in here. Yes!' She walked over to the bookshelves. 'Here she is—so sad she's no longer with us; she was lovely in every way.' She lifted the silver-framed photo off the shelf and handed it to Chattie.

'Goodness me,' she went on as Chattie studied the fair woman in the photo who looked a lot like Mark, pictured with a tall man who reminded her of Steve, 'would you believe I was at Mark's christening?' she confided to Chattie with a twinkle.

Chattie smiled.

'And there used to be one of Steve's wedding,' Joan went on, 'but I'd be surprised if he allowed her to keep it—oh, yes!' She plucked a photo that Chattie hadn't previously noticed from behind an ornament.

Chattie's lips parted. 'Steve—has been married?'

'Yes, it didn't work out, though, and they're divorced. She was very beautiful but very much a city girl and she just didn't take to life out here. She often used to accuse him of having a one-track mind—cattle, cattle, cattle.'

It was as if a blinding light suddenly illuminated the dark corners of Chattie's mind—several blinding lights. Steve Kinane had thought she was accusing him of the same thing last night, and earlier he might have overheard her comment on the subject of his not being married—was that why Merlene had looked embarrassed? Just about to be caught discussing his private life by the boss might well do it.

She swallowed. 'I didn't know.'

'I'm sure it's all behind him now, although he hasn't taken the plunge again and it's been quite a while since they parted—years, actually—and there have been plenty who would have loved to attach themselves to him.'

Chattie studied the stunning girl on Steve's arm, the way he was looking down at her, then handed the picture back.

'Mrs Jackson, would you like a cup of tea? And perhaps a sandwich? I'd be happy to bring it to your room.'

Joan Jackson beamed at Chattie. 'That would be so kind, my dear! I don't get these wretched headaches often, but when I do...!'

But as she cut up the sandwiches and brewed some tea all Chattie could think of was Steve Kinane's failed marriage and the way he'd been looking down at his bride.

* * *

At six o'clock drinks were in progress in the lounge, the dining room was candlelit and resplendent, the kitchen was a model of good management—and the lights went off.

'Power failure,' Merlene said laconically. 'Happens all the time out here.'

'You're joking!' Chattie stared at her through the gloom. 'There are no storms in the offing, are there?' she asked nervously.

'No. It isn't only storms that do it, though.'

'What is wrong with this day? It seems determined to…flatten me!'

Steve came into the kitchen. 'We have a back-up generator, Chattie, don't panic.' He strode out of the back door.

Chattie took several deep breaths. 'I'm not panicking,' she assured Merlene. 'Well, only slightly.'

'We've still got the stove.' Merlene pointed to the wood-burning range. 'It's one reason why they kept it.'

Chattie nodded but thought of the use she'd planned to make of the microwave, the toaster, the electric coffee machine, the electric blender, and felt a little faint. 'How long does it take to get the generator going?'

'No time at all, usually.' Merlene shrugged. 'But I'll get some candles and paraffin lamps just to be on the safe side.'

The words struck a little chill in Chattie and, sure enough, fifteen minutes later Steve came back into the kitchen wiping his hands on a rag and looking grim.

'Don't tell me!' Chattie pleaded.

'Sorry, but the bloody thing has blown a fuse and it's short-circuited completely. It's a major repair job now that'll take hours. Look—' he looked around '—just size things down to what's ready, they'll understand, and I'll send Harriet in to give you a hand.'

Merlene snorted but Chattie had taken several deep breaths.

She said. 'If Harriet would help with the serving, we'd be most grateful, but I will not allow this day to defeat me even though it's been trying to *do* so all day!' She raised her chin. 'Please tell everyone dinner will be delayed by about half an hour but otherwise everything is fine.'

'Chattie—'

Steve Kinane paused and sighed as he observed his housekeeper. She'd chosen to wear slim floral trousers on a white background with an apple-green shirt. Over it, at the moment, she had a clear plastic apron, her hair was drawn back in a bunch and her feet were encased in green leather flat shoes. There could be no mistaking her determination from her expression, but she was so lovely at the same time, she reminded him of an avenging goddess of the very slim, very young variety.

'Hang on,' he said abruptly, and walked through to the dining room. He came back minutes later with two glasses of champagne, one of which he handed to her, the other to Merlene.

'There you go, troops,' he said with a wicked little smile. 'That should ease the pain a bit.'

'Why, thank you!' Chattie said in a genuine rush of good cheer. 'That's the best thing that's happened to me all day!' She raised her glass to toast him. 'Off you go, then; we'll be fine now!'

* * *

And, in due course, a delicate asparagus soup was served, followed by a magnificent beef Wellington and vegetables including cauliflower au gratin. And for dessert, a baked lemon cheesecake, topped with glacé lemon slices and a fruit salad, was served with hand-beaten cream.

By the time the dessert had gone into the dining room—Harriet had done all the ferrying in and out of food and dishes and tried to be as helpful as possible—the kitchen resembled a battlefield and Merlene was swearing audibly because she couldn't locate the manual coffee grinder.

'How are we going to grind these damn beans? I know there's one somewhere!'

'Merlene,' Chattie said, sinking into a chair, 'I'll let you into a little secret. A dash of something like Tia Maria gives a whole new meaning to instant coffee. Glory be—let there be light!' she added as the lights came on. Then she looked around and started to giggle. 'Let's go back to candles!'

Steve came in at that moment and looked around ruefully, and as the lights went out again said, 'That was a false alarm, thankfully, I agree with you. Uh—your presence is required in the dining room, Miss Winslow.'

Chattie put her hands to her cheeks, which were shiny with perspiration, touched her hair and knew it to be out of control, looked at her fingernails, and said decidedly, 'No way!'

'Then I'll bring them in here,' he murmured.

'Who?'

'The shire chairman and his lady—they're very desirous of making your acquaintance.'

'Don't you dare!' Chattie and Merlene chorused, with Merlene adding, 'Wash your hands, spit on your eyebrows, push your fingers through your hair, Chattie, but don't let 'em see this mess—I'll never live it down. And take your apron off,' she recommended.

Chattie did it all, even to licking a fingertip and smoothing her eyebrows, although she favoured Steve Kinane with a dark glance along the way. 'This is blackmail.'

'You'll probably change your mind when you hear what they have to say. One thing, don't accept any job offers—I wouldn't appreciate you leaving me in the lurch.'

'Well, ma'am,' the shire chairman, who was a large man with a large belly, said on Chattie's arrival in the dining room, and paused to do a double take, 'I have to tell you, you are going to make some lucky man a magnificent wife and I really would like to introduce you to my son!' He turned to his wife. 'Wouldn't you, Beryl?'

Beryl nodded enthusiastically. Ray Cook, Jack Barlow and John Jackson raised their glasses in heartfelt agreement, causing Harriet Barlow to look oddly thoughtful—and Sasha Kelly to look bored to tears. But the other women seconded this sentiment heartily and insisted Chattie sit down with them for a moment.

Two hours later when those driving had gone home and those staying had all gone to bed, Steve found his housekeeper asleep at the dining-room table.

She'd obviously been setting it for breakfast, but she

was now sitting at it with her head on her arms and dead to the world.

He surveyed her for a moment, and then said her name.

No response.

'Well, I can't leave you here all night,' he murmured wryly, and carefully manoeuvred her out of the chair and into his arms. She didn't wake as he carried her to her bedroom, and he quietly recommended to Rich to think twice about attacking him.

Then he went to put Chattie down on the bed, but she made a murmur of dissent and cuddled up against him with her arms around his neck, so he sat down on the bed with her in his lap instead. 'Chattie?'

'Mmm?' Her lashes fluttered but she was only half awake and she rubbed her cheek against his shoulder with a sigh of pleasure, and closed her eyes again.

A nerve flickered in his jaw as he looked down at the curvy, half-folded length of her. She was completely relaxed and felt soft and boneless against him. Her hair smelt of lemons, there was a streak of gravy down her blouse and a blob of blueberry on one knee of her trousers. She'd abandoned her shoes somewhere along the line.

But despite her exertions or even because of them—did it add a strength of character that made her irresistible?—she was quite lovely. Smooth-skinned, beautifully curved, delicately tinted—and from nowhere a vision came to Steve Kinane of the shire chairman's son, Ryan.

He grimaced at the thought. Ryan Winters was a brawny, good-looking young man of considerable ego. He was also considered the local stud, but had all the finesse of a front-row forward and it was simply un-thinkable to imagine Charlotte Winslow in his arms.

Come to that, he thought grimly, he would have difficulty imagining her in anyone's arms but his own and therein lay a contretemps of the highest order for him.

Not only on account of her connection with his brother, he acknowledged, but because he'd consid-ered himself immune from emotional entanglements now…

So how the hell, he asked himself, had he fallen for a girl who cherished the same negative sentiments about his state of mind as his ex-wife had?

Chattie moved in his arms, said drowsily, 'This is so nice after a hard day at the office!' And opened her eyes.

For a moment nothing registered in their grey depths, then comprehension dawned, consternation be-came shock and shock was coupled with deep embar-rassment.

'Pardon me,' she whispered, going scarlet and scrambling to sit up. 'I…I don't know what you must think! I didn't realize it was you. I…' She got unsteadily to her feet at the same time as she anxiously patted her blouse into place, checked the buttons and smoothed her trousers. 'I am sorry but I guess I was overtired—'

'Or you thought I was Mark?' he suggested dryly.

'I'm not sure what I thought—' She stopped abruptly and her eyes widened.

'Unless you make a habit of it.'

'What?'

'Enjoying any man's arms around you,' he said flatly.

Indignation rushed to the surface. 'I do not!' she denied. 'How can you say that? You know, there are times when I quite like you, Steve Kinane, and times when you make it impossible!'

He shrugged. 'Then we'll have to go with the Mark scenario.'

It occurred to Chattie in a blinding instant that there was another scenario. Subconsciously she'd known all along it was Steve, and, again subconsciously, had felt safe with him yet again. Safe—*and as if she belonged in his arms...*

'I think,' she said, and patted her cheeks to hide her mortification, 'we should put it down to a long—extremely fraught, in fact—day. That's all.' She tilted her chin.

He smiled unexpectedly, and briefly. 'You'll be asking for danger money next.'

'I'm not saying it was above or beyond anything I expected to be called upon to do!' she countered with a flash of irritation. 'I'm using it to explain—oh, what's the use?' She turned away and sniffed. 'I think I better go to bed,' she said huskily, 'since we're destined to misunderstand each other completely, by the look of it.'

The moments ticked by as he said nothing and something compelled her to turn back. And she became conscious as they stared at each other of a rising tide between them of something elementary, something dangerous and disturbing but powerful at the same time. Like the peril of an emotional and physical storm about to break between them whether they liked it or not, whether they could rationalize it or not—and she certainly couldn't.

Because there was no way she felt safe with Steve Kinane at that moment. No way to guarantee that those dangerous, disturbing sensations racing through her at the way he was looking at her wouldn't push her into his arms unsure if she loved him or hated him but unable to resist him…

Her lips parted and her eyes widened in a stunned reaction. Never before in her life had a man stirred her like this for one thing, but to be unsure whether she hated him—or *loved* him, to have that spring into her mind was unbelievable.

He stood up and cut the eye contact. 'Might be a good idea for both of us to go to bed, but please don't think I haven't appreciated your efforts today. Even Slim would have been proud of you and he has very high standards. By the way, the bypass operation was successful and he's resting comfortably.'

It seemed to Chattie that her tongue was stuck to the roof of her mouth for some strange reason, so she swallowed visibly. 'That's good news.'

'Yes. Goodnight.'

She stared at the door after he'd closed it behind him, and wondered if she was going mad.

This roundabout of physical attraction, of liking, even respecting at times, and certainly feeling safe with Steve Kinane, then disliking him intensely, was impossible.

She shivered and got ready for bed distractedly. As she slid under the rose-red eiderdown it occurred to her that she might never get this man out of her system because, not only he, but also his damn cattle station was getting under her skin.

Face it, Chattie, she told herself, this would be a very fulfilling lifestyle for you, but how could it ever be?

Then another thought crept into her mind. She might not have had time to assess the impact it had had on her, but she couldn't get Steve Kinane's wedding photo out of her mind. Or the conviction that he'd been deeply in love with his bride.

CHAPTER SEVEN

CHATTIE was making an omelette for breakfast the next morning—full power had been restored—when someone came into the kitchen through the back door. Because it was very early, too early for Merlene normally and she was sure it had to be Steve, Chattie dropped the bowl and the egg, milk, mushrooms and finely diced onions spread in a wide, yellow-and-black-dotted stain across the floor.

It was Merlene, however, who stopped at the outer edge of the stain, looked down at it, then looked across at Chattie standing pale and transfixed. 'You OK, kid?'

'I'm jittery,' Chattie confessed ruefully. 'I don't know why but I feel as if something terrible is going to happen and it's all my fault.'

'Bloody hell,' Merlene replied.

Chattie grimaced. 'Don't take any notice of me, it will pass. Could you hand me a cloth?'

'What will pass?' It *was* Steve who came in this time, from the opposite direction. He also stopped at the outer edge of the stain, studied it, then studied Chattie and finally raised an eyebrow at Merlene.

'Chattie reckons the world's about to end and it's all her fault,' Merlene explained.

Sheer amusement lit his eyes but he said gravely to Merlene, 'Would you present my compliments to Miss Winslow? Would you also tell her that I had hoped to catch her before she started breakfast, to apprise her that she doesn't have to do a thing because I've organized a barbecue breakfast for the entire present population of Mount Helena down at the bunkhouse?'

'Good thinking, boss!' Merlene applauded. 'Seems to me our young godsend may have stretched herself a wee bit too far over the last couple of days.'

'I told her not to—' Steve started to say exasperatedly but concluded, 'Well, be that as it may, how does she respond?'

Chattie said it in her mind but the words echoed like a foghorn so it seemed impossible that the other two wouldn't hear—That has nothing to do with it! I'm bothered and bewildered because I don't know what's going on between, to be precise, Charlotte Winslow, spinster, and Steve Kinane, divorcee.

'She's really got the wobblies,' Merlene said for her after a moment, 'but I'll accept on her behalf. Why don't you take her out to…smell the flowers or something while I clean up the mess? Looks like she could do with it.'

Chattie came to life. 'Thanks, but that won't be necessary—I was only joking.'

Steve started to say something but the phone rang. Merlene picked it up, then handed it to him. 'Jack. He's got a bit of a problem.'

Steve listened for a couple of moments, then said down the line, 'I'll be there in five.' He handed the phone back to Merlene. 'You're in charge of getting this mob down to the bunkhouse, mate, and you—' he turned to Chattie '—can come with me.'

'Why? What's happened? Why do you need me?' Chattie asked dazedly.

'I do, that's all. Out you go.' He pushed her in the direction of the back door.

She was about to protest vigorously but she caught sight of Merlene out of the corner of her eye. And Merlene was clearly indicating by way of her thumb that Chattie should do as she was told.

'I still don't understand,' Chattie said breathlessly once she was in the Range Rover and Steve was climbing in beside her. Then her eyes grew suddenly fearful. 'It's not anything to do with Brett, is it?'

He switched the motor on and revved the engine. 'No, he's fine as far as I know. My favourite horse has got herself cast in her box.'

'Cast?' she repeated. 'What does that mean?'

'That she lay down or rolled over too close to the wall and now she's got no space to push off so she can't get up.'

'Why doesn't she just roll over again?'

'Sometimes that logic doesn't occur to a horse,' he said wryly. 'Sometimes they get so frightened they don't think straight. Sometimes, in their struggles, they really get themselves wedged in.'

Chattie's eyes all but stood out on stalks. 'You're not expecting me to help you, are you? I don't know a thing about horses!'

'No, I'm not expecting you to help,' he replied, ruefully this time. 'Just thought it would be good for you to get out and about a bit. Can't have my ace housekeeper worried about the end of the world.'

So that's the way it's going to be, Chattie thought as she stared down at her hands and the shiny red apple in them that she'd plucked from the fruit bowl while being propelled out of the kitchen. Swept under the carpet, unless I was imagining all sorts of weird things last night.

Then the supreme irony of that thought came to her. He was doing precisely what she'd tried to do after he'd kissed her on the night of the storm.

'You don't wish to comment?' he said.

She shook her head. 'But thanks for organizing me out of breakfast.'

'What else were we talking about?'

Chattie gazed at him coolly. 'I have no idea.'

'Uh-oh, one of those impasses.' His lips twisted

'Those?' she queried.

'Of the domestic dispute variety,' he quipped, and pulled to a stop in front of the stables. 'OK, let's see what we can do.'

Chattie stayed where she was with surprise and growing indignation colouring her expression.

'I get it,' he drawled. 'You're thinking MEN, in capital letters, but that's what I meant. I was thinking, WOMEN—along the same lines.'

'You know what I think? That you're one of those impossibly bright and bushy early morning people sent to torment the life out of the rest of the planet!' she retorted, and got out of the vehicle to close her door with a bang.

Steve Kinane flinched but a shrill whinny split the air and he turned away from the car immediately.

The scene inside the stables was horrifying—to Chattie at least.

Steve's favourite horse was a chestnut filly with one white sock and a white blaze. Sweat had darkened her coat and panic was sending tremors through her as she lay on her side wedged against the back wall of the stall.

'Every time we go near her,' Jack Barlow said, 'she tries to thrash about but she can't get over and I'm afraid she's going to injure herself. Like that,' he added as the filly strove mightily and convulsively to get to her feet to no avail.

'Get a couple of slings,' Steve ordered, then stepped into the stall and approached the horse's head. Chattie held her breath but immediately his tone changed as he knelt down beside the filly.

'Daisy, my darling,' he said soothingly, 'how did you get yourself into this mess?' He rubbed her neck and stroked her nose.

As Chattie watched in wonderment the horse relaxed, almost with a very human sigh of relief, and as Steve kept on talking to her and rubbing her he directed traffic with his other hand until Jack and one of the hands were in the positions he wanted them. Then, and Chattie wasn't quite sure how they did it, with one concerted movement they all heaved, Daisy flailed her legs and, scattering Jack and the hand, plunged to her feet.

She then, perhaps in an excess of exuberance at being freed, kicked out at the wall with both back legs.

Jack swore as he dodged just in time. At the same time Steve slipped a headstall onto her and admonished her with a grin. 'If you weren't such a darn good racehorse and hadn't just had a nasty experience, Miss Daisy, that kind of behaviour would not be overlooked.'

Daisy harrumphed and stuck her nose lovingly into his armpit. Steve submitted to this treatment for a couple of minutes, then he handed her over to Bill, the hand, and gave her a thorough running-over with his hands.

'Doesn't appear to be any damage but just trot her up and down a couple of times.'

Bill led the filly out into the central passageway and obliged while Jack and Steve studied her action.

'I reckon she's fine,' Jack said, and they all burst out laughing as Daisy turned her head as she passed Chattie and tried to pinch the apple out of her hand.

But instead of getting a fright Chattie was enchanted, and asked if she could feed it to the horse.

'Bite off bits and just lay them in your palm,' Steve said.

She did so and felt Daisy's velvety muzzle tickling her hand. Moreover, once the apple was consumed, she petted the horse before finally turning to Steve and saying, 'I don't know why I haven't had anything to do with horses! I'd love to learn to ride.'

'Yes, well, they are big and they do kick and bite sometimes,' Steve said and looked at her thoughtfully for a long moment. Then, 'OK, Bill, you can put her out in the paddock.' They strolled outside.

'Tell me a bit more about her,' Chattie invited as they leant against the Range Rover in the early morning sunlight.

'Her racing name is Miss Daisy. She's three years old and she's already won half a million dollars.'

'Wow! But do you…you don't train her yourself, do you?'

'No, but we own her dam, she was born and reared here, and she comes back here between preparations to spell.'

'So you've known her since the day she was born? That explains it,' Chattie murmured.

He cocked an eyebrow at her.

'Why she trusts you so much—is what I mean.'

He shrugged. 'Possibly. There's also a key to handling bright, spirited, flighty young things of the female persuasion. You need to kid to them a bit, you need to get them to trust you and you need them to know that when you put your foot down, that's it.'

'Only of the female persuasion?' Chattie asked gravely, then laughed with delight as Miss Daisy was released into the paddock where she put on a very spirited bucking exhibition before settling down and approaching the feed bin Bill had hooked over the fence rail.

'Colts,' Steve said, 'often need more authority, less kidding to.'

'I'm glad you qualified that very sexist statement, otherwise I could have got quite the wrong impression of you!' But her eyes were still dancing.

'In amongst all the other wrong impressions you have of me?' he queried.

'I was joking.' She sobered completely, and sighed.

He folded his arms and leant back against the Range Rover. Unlike her he wore no jumper against the chill of the air although they both wore jeans. And, unlike her earlier sentiments on the subject of men in general and Steve Kinane in particular, she was once again on the roundabout.

She'd started out the day feeling nervous and beleaguered because of him. Then she'd been most impressed by his physical and mental skills with Miss

Daisy, but in between she'd been thoroughly annoyed with him—even slamming his car door.

Now, though, she had no idea where she stood. Respect, admiration, and enjoyment of his company—all those things were there. There was also a whole lot about him she didn't know, not to mention that mixture of danger and delight he could arouse in her.

'Chattie—' she looked up to meet his dark gaze, and as it roamed briefly up and down her figure she literally experienced one of those dangerous moments '—tell me a couple of things. What will you do when you go back to Brisbane?'

Surprise caused her eyes to widen. 'Go back to my college, of course.'

'Will that be easy? And enjoyable?'

She looked around, shielding her eyes from the sun as she did so. And once again it swooped on her like a bird falling through the sky onto its prey—that Mount Helena was becoming more fascinating to her with every passing day.

She'd come to love the wide open spaces. She stood on her veranda every morning feeling liberated as she looked around. Feeling adventurous and with her painter's eye glorying in the colours and the width, depth and height of the canvas before her.

She also felt as if she'd grown, not physically but internally, with the job she was doing, the challenges she was meeting. And, not that she wanted to look forward to a career of housekeeping, but the life she was living was much more satisfying than her previous existence of teaching in a city, she realized.

Hang on right there, she cautioned herself, and the bird of her imagination soared back skywards out of reach... I can't stay on here after Bridget's news gets out so why am I even contemplating it?

'Chattie?'

She cleared her throat, then replied with a shrug, 'I'm a working girl.'

'Will you stay on here until the end of your holidays? That's about another two weeks, by my estimation.'

'I...' She paused and started to colour beneath his assessing gaze. 'No.'

'Why not?'

'Well—' she spread her hands and tried to think coherently '—you're not quite so much in the lurch now. Surely you could get a replacement for Slim from a pastoral agency? I don't know how long it will take him to recuperate, but if it's longer than two weeks you'll have to anyway.'

'What about Mark?'

'What about him?' she said absently, because her thoughts couldn't have been further from Mark Kinane or Bridget for that matter.

'Isn't he your *raison d'être* for being here in the first place?' he asked with palpable irony. 'Or are you starting to forget all about my brother, Chattie?'

She closed her eyes. 'No.'

'You don't lie very well.'

She bit her lip.

'Last night,' he said, 'you—'

'Please don't,' she whispered.

'Just another attack of involuntary thoughtlessness?' he suggested dryly.

Her lashes fluttered up to see he was focused on her intently.

'Which leads me to wonder if that's why you're going to go—because you can't help yourself with me. But the thing is, I have the same problem, so you would imagine it would make us—square.'

'Steve…' she took a shaken breath '…I—'

'No, Chattie, enough of this,' he said roughly, and took her in his arms. 'I don't know what game the hell you're playing but, the fact is, I don't care. Because sparks flew between us almost from the moment we met and I won't rest until you're honest about it.'

He lowered his mouth to hers.

'You promised you wouldn't do this,' she protested.

'To all intents and purposes the house party is over—and as you pointed out yourself I'm no longer completely in the lurch,' he growled against her lips.

'But anybody could see us!'

'Let 'em,' he said contemptuously. 'I've spent all bloody night wondering about you and how you like to be made love to. And you, my dear, were the one who fell asleep at the dining room table then didn't want me to let you go.'

Tears of confusion, of frustration, beaded her lashes but she blinked them away. 'I'm sorry,' she said huskily. 'I just…I just don't know what to say any more.'

'Good. Don't say a thing, then. Unless you'd like to tell me how you do like it.'

But he didn't give her a chance. He kissed the one tear that had escaped, then claimed her mouth possessively and hungrily.

When they finally drew apart, Chattie felt as if she'd come as close to being made love to as was possible without it actually happening. Her lips were bruised but her body was alive and singing with the desire that was coursing through her veins. She felt alive and intoxicated with the feel and the taste of him. She felt as if she was on a new threshold, but once again, as if she belonged in his arms,

'Anything thoughtless about that?' he queried.

'No. It's…lovely,' she admitted raggedly.

'Are you wearing a colourful bra?' he asked, with his hands beneath her jumper.

For a moment she couldn't remember what bra she was wearing. 'Why?'

'The one I saw a couple of nights ago was like no other I've seen.'

'I make my own bras,' she murmured and shivered as his fingers found her nipples.

'Is there anything you can't do?' he queried with a smile in his eyes.

'Cope with thunderstorms.'

'Will you stay on now? I'll see if I can organize a thunder-free period for the next two weeks.'

He was massaging her nipples with his thumbs and it was sending quivering tendrils of sheer delight to the pit of her stomach, and an intimation of further delight she could only marvel at with a breathless little gasp.

'Chattie?' he said softly but insistently.

That was when they heard hurried footsteps crunching along the gravel path from the stables.

She froze and Steve removed his hands from her breasts, pulled her jumper down decorously but kept her in his arms as he turned his head to look over the bonnet of the Range Rover to see who it was.

It was Jack Barlow, coming to a sudden stop. 'Par-

don me,' he said in some confusion. 'I didn't realize—
that is to say I...didn't realize—'

'That's OK,' Steve said abruptly. 'Got a problem?'

Jack scratched his head as if he was still getting to
grips with the scene he was witnessing, then he looked
urgent. 'You could say so. A chopper's come down
on the property—not ours. Some guys surveying who
strayed off course and then suffered a mechanical failure. The pilot's broken his leg—'

Steve swore and released Chattie. 'Badly?' he queried tersely.

Jack nodded. 'Compound fracture, by the sound of
it. We're going to have to organize a search-and-
rescue mission pronto.'

'One of those days,' Steve said dryly and turned
back to Chattie. Could—' he paused '—could I ask
you to handle the breakup of the house party?'

'Of course. Is there anything else I can do?' she
asked anxiously.

'No, but thanks. Just—don't do anything I
wouldn't,' he said and kissed her hair. 'Promise?'

She swallowed. 'I promise.'

'That's my girl.'

The news of the helicopter crash saw the house party
break up rather quickly. All able-bodied men were seconded to the search, although John Jackson flew his
wife home first.

Chattie received a warm hug from Joan Jackson and
another from Lucy Cook. Sasha Kelly merely murmured goodbye in a languid manner. Harriet was on
hand to farewell the guests, and, slightly to Chattie's

surprise, suggested they have a cup of coffee once everyone had left.

Then again, she thought, Harriet had been really helpful as well as friendly the previous evening, so why not?

'I must say—' Harriet poured two steaming mugs '—you were inspired last night, Chattie.'

'Thanks. And thanks for your help.'

'Actually—' Harriet eyed Chattie over her mug '—you're exactly what Steve needs.'

Chattie went still. 'What do you mean?' Then enlightenment dawned. 'Jack didn't waste any time, did he?'

'No, he didn't.' But Harriet looked entirely unembarrassed. 'However, there is one thing you should know. Steve's been a different person since his wife, Nadine, left him. It hardened him and made him, well, pretty cynical about marriage.'

So that was her name: Nadine.

'Harriet,' Chattie said carefully, 'why are you telling me this?'

'Two reasons, I guess. It might help you to understand when you run into that wall of cynicism, as you're bound to. And he's done an awful lot for me so I wouldn't like to see him get hurt again.'

Chattie stared into Harriet's blue eyes and saw genuine concern. She looked away. 'Harriet, we've only known each other for such a short time it's impossible to say what will happen.'

'According to Jack all things looked possible this morning! And I get the feeling the mild interest Steve may have had in Sasha Kelly has—' Harriet theatrically thumped her palm on the table '—died.'

Chattie blinked.

'He was quite cool towards her when she tried to be—how can I say it?—possessive, last night,' Harriet added.

'Really? I—'

'And I believe you had a little run-in with her yourself?'

'Yes. Yes, I did.'

'Well, then.' Harriet looked complacent. 'Don't tell me you don't like it out here? You've fitted in so damn well, it's amazing. That is something Nadine did not do.'

Chattie simply couldn't help herself. 'Why did they marry, then?'

Harriet raised her eyebrows expressively. 'You should have seen her.' She shrugged. 'To all intents and purposes they made a fantastic couple but the isolation got to her. Actually, I think what really got to her was the fact that Steve could afford to have a full-time manager so they could have lived anywhere, but he wouldn't even contemplate it. He loves this place and this lifestyle.'

Chattie finished her coffee and rose, prey to a whole series of conflicting emotions. What would happen at the end of two weeks if she stayed? She had no doubt they would not be able to resist each other for much longer...

She stared out over the paddocks. Even without the complication of Bridget, would there be a future for her with Steve? Or, did he have in mind an affair for only as long as their passion lasted? Which led directly on to, she thought, was Harriet right about the cynicism he'd been left with towards marriage?

How *could* she leave Bridget out of the equation, though? She sighed inwardly and turned back to Harriet.

'Would you have any idea where Mark is?'

Harriet looked surprised. 'None. Why?'

'I—just wondered. Do you—obviously you know his ex-fiancée?'

Harriet shook her head. 'Never met her, none of us did, although I believe her name was Bryony. It was very much a uni kind of crush, from what I could gather.'

'So you don't think he's...gone back to her?'

Harriet waved a hand. 'Haven't a clue. Why?'

'Oh, nothing. Well...' Chattie shrugged '...that's how I came to be here in the first place—because I'd met Mark.'

The other girl wrinkled her nose. 'Forget about Mark. He's got a whole lot of growing up to do. I would have thought,' she added with a frown, 'Steve had quite wiped Mark from your mind.'

'You would be quite right,' Chattie replied with a burst of somewhat bitter honesty at the same time as Merlene came out onto the veranda.

They both turned to her. 'You got a sister called Bridget, Chattie?'

'Yes! Why?' Chattie sat up urgently.

'She's on the blower.'

'Oh, excuse me, Harriet—'

'Don't mind me, I'm about to go home anyway. Just remember what I said!'

'Bridget, it's me,' Chattie said into the kitchen connection. 'Are you all right?' She listened for about half a minute with her mouth falling open, then said, *'What?'*

Two minutes later she put the phone down and dropped her head into her hands in disbelief.

'Everything OK?' Merlene enquired.

'No. Well. My sister is on her way here. She's hitched a lift with a friend of a friend who is flying his light plane up to Longreach.'

'Is that such a disaster?' Merlene asked curiously.

'You have no idea,' Chattie said slowly. 'They expect to be here about mid-afternoon. Apparently this guy has flown into Helena before. He…' she paused *'he's* a friend of Mark's and he has a courier-run contract.'

'Oh, that'd be Andrew Watson,' Merlene said blithely. 'He often drops in with urgent packages. I still don't see what the problem is. The more the merrier!' she added jovially.

Chattie closed her eyes. 'I just hope he has plenty of airsick bags.'

CHAPTER EIGHT

OF COURSE it couldn't have happened any other way, Chattie marvelled bitterly.

Steve came back after the search-and-rescue operation had been successfully concluded and pulled the Range Rover up at the garden fence at the same time as Andrew Watson touched his smart little plane down on the airstrip.

Chattie had been alerted to its arrival when he'd buzzed the homestead and was waiting beside the strip.

Steve walked over to her with a frown as he observed the Watson Courier logo as the plane turned and taxied back.

'I'm not expecting anything,' he said. 'Something I don't know about?'

She took a deep breath. 'Yes. But I can explain.'

He looked down into her grey eyes and his frown grew. 'Like what?'

Chattie made a mental note to preserve how she and Steve Kinane had been in each other's arms that morning, to capture it and store it in her heart, because she was deadly afraid she might never be so close to him again.

'My sister,' she said.

'Your...' He paused as the plane stopped, the door opened, the steps lowered and Andrew Watson, who was a burly young man in his mid-twenties, got out.

Then he turned back to hand someone down and Bridget appeared, looking a wreck. She was pale, her dark hair was mussed and her clothes crumpled and entirely inappropriate—a filmy see-through skirt and a halter-neck top. She was also not too steady on her feet.

'That's your sister?' Steve said incredulously.

Chattie didn't answer. She went up to Bridget and put her arms around her. 'Bridge, you shouldn't have! Are you all right?'

'She's been a bit sick,' Andrew said. 'She's been very sick,' he amended with a rueful glance at Steve over his shoulder, 'but I guess that's normal. Took my wife the same way.'

Chattie blinked at him. 'You know?'

Bridget raised her head. 'I told him.' She cleared her throat. 'He needed to know why I have to find Mark. And,' she said, with tears falling down her cheeks, 'I don't care who knows now because I love Mark deeply, I'm having his baby and that's that.'

Steve Kinane froze.

'So all is explained,' he said.

Chattie swallowed nervously. It was an hour or so later. Bridget had been restored with a light snack and was fast asleep in Chattie's room. Seeing how exhausted she was, Chattie hadn't pressed for more of an explanation than the one Bridget had repeated several times—it had just come to her that she couldn't sit around twiddling her thumbs any longer, that she wasn't ashamed of being pregnant or of loving Mark Kinane.

Steve had been completely inscrutable on being introduced, but not unkind. He'd welcomed Bridget to Mount Helena and suggested that she have a rest before they discussed anything.

He'd then taken Andrew aside, leaving Chattie to shepherd her sister inside. A few minutes later, the plane had taken off and Chattie had heard Steve drive away.

Fortunately, Merlene had been down at the bunkhouse so no explanations for the state of her sister had had to be made immediately.

Then Steve had come home and Chattie had girded her loins, and gone to find him.

He'd been in the lounge, pouring a drink, and he'd accorded her another inscrutable glance but opened a bottle of wine.

It was as he'd handed her the glass that he'd made his comment about all being explained.

She took the glass he handed her and sat down because her legs felt like jelly.

'You don't know how many times I was on the verge of telling you,' she said, 'but you—' She gestured helplessly.

He sat down opposite, his eyes hard and cool. 'So it's my fault—is that what you're saying?'

She took a fortifying sip. 'No. Well, you made your sentiments so plain about your brother being trapped into marriage I—look, may I start at the beginning?'

'Be my guest,' he said dryly.

She put her glass down and twined her fingers. Ten minutes later she'd told him everything. How Bridget had depended on her since they'd been orphaned, how Bridget and Mark had met, the course of their affair and why, since Bridget was not only pregnant but the person she was anyway, she, Chattie, had decided to track Mark down for her.

'I see.' Steve swirled his drink. 'And what do you think Mark's reaction to this news will be?'

'I…I have no idea. But whatever happens for them, this baby deserves his support, and deserves, at least, to know who its father is.'

'Can we be quite sure Mark is the father?'

Chattie looked directly into his eyes with a fighting little glint in hers. 'I have no doubt whatsoever.'

'It's no good getting angry with me, Chattie,' he advised.

She stood up and paced across the room restlessly. 'Then don't say things like that.'

'I—or Mark, anyway—has every right to be sure this is his child. Incidentally, did you not try to talk any sense into your sister?' he queried.

'I tried my level best,' she replied grimly. Then she sighed. 'If you ever get to know Bridget any better you'll…well, she's not very wise at times. That doesn't mean to say she isn't warm, loyal and wonderful.'

'All of which Mark managed to walk away from with little difficulty, apparently,' he said with considerable irony.

'Bridget blames you for that.' Chattie bit her lip. 'Look, I don't know one way or the other—'

'You don't know?' he shot at her savagely.

Chattie gestured defensively. 'I have come to wonder about it,' she said, 'but the fact of the matter is, Bridget is convinced—from what Mark told her, obviously—that he has an inferiority complex, that he's all mixed-up and that he had to break up with her because you ordered him home.'

'How convenient,' he said scathingly.

'You mean for Mark?' she asked uncertainly.

'I mean for Mark,' he agreed. 'Sit down, Chattie,' he ordered. 'I'm getting a stiff neck watching you pace around.'

She took a breath and was on the verge of telling him to go to hell but changed her mind.

'All right.' He finished his drink. 'Since I'm the villain of the piece, let me tell you this. My mother tried for years to have another child after I was born. She didn't succeed until ten years later and after several miscarriages and two live births, but she lost both of them. I think she'd almost given up hope. Then Mark came along and she doted on him and was extremely protective. Not only that, she was very artistic and he seemed to inherit it.

'My father,' he said, 'resented the way she pampered him, which made for an uncomfortable upbringing for Mark and therein do lie the seeds of his restlessness. Nevertheless, I have never,' he said with emphasis, 'tried to make a cattleman out of Mark. Yes, when I need help, I have no conscience about roping him in and, to be honest, I don't think it does him any harm to be reminded where his bread comes from. But I will be only too happy for Mark to find his place in life, whatever it is.'

Chattie looked troubled.

'It could be we're in the same boat with our siblings,' Steve said after a moment.

She had to agree.

'And, contrary to what you may have decided,

Mark's happiness does matter to me.' He engaged her gaze deliberately and added, 'What I can't understand—OK, I may have contributed at the start—but how could you have deceived me for so long, Chattie?'

She stared into his dark eyes and shivered because she couldn't doubt he was deeply angry.

'My first concern had to be my sister,' she said quietly. 'I wasn't to know what kind of power you wielded over Mark or what lengths you'd go to protect him from this.'

'Do you think he's ready for marriage and children?' he fired at her.

Chattie looked helpless. 'I don't know. I mean, I liked him but, to be honest, I think they're two of a kind. Impetuous, immature—'

'Did you think he was as deeply in love with Bridget as she feels she is with him?'

'He certainly appeared to be, although...' She paused.

'Go on.'

'You haven't seen her at her best,' Chattie said. 'She is—gorgeous.'

Steve sat back. 'That goes without saying. What does she do? Anything?'

Chattie swallowed her ire. 'She's training to be a model.'

He lifted an eyebrow. 'I might have known. So the practical, down-to-earth genes bypassed her?'

'She is only nineteen,' Chattie said defensively. 'Look, this has happened. Aren't we better off working out what's best to be done rather than indulging in an orgy of recriminations? Believe me, it's no more my fault than it is yours!'

'So what are you expecting? That I drag Mark to the altar for you?'

'No,' Chattie cried exasperatedly, 'not if he has to be dragged! But some help, some support for Mark's child, some recognition.'

'In the form of dollars and cents?'

Chattie had picked up her glass but she put it down with a snap and went white. 'I can't believe you said that!'

'No? That's strange,' he drawled. 'You believe a lot of other things about me. You obviously cherish the suspicion that I'm some kind of monster, not to be trusted, not to be dealt with in honesty—no wonder you had such a battle with yourself when it came to being intimate with me.'

She went from white to pink beneath his intimately assessing gaze that stripped away her clothes and dwelt, reminiscently, on her breasts.

Nor was it a charge she could deny. 'Bridget is the only family I have,' she said wearily, then frowned. 'All right, I know this has come as a shock to you. When I found out I was—distraught. But if Mark and Bridget don't get together, by far the largest part of this burden will always be on her.'

'If they don't get together, the only real support we'll be able to give her is monetary,' he pointed out and stopped rather abruptly.

'What?' Chattie whispered, because of the way he was looking at her. As if he was honed in on her and her alone but in a curiously predatory manner.

'There is another way,' he said at last.

She blinked at him.

'You could marry me, Chattie Winslow.'

She gasped and for a moment the room spun round.

'What's so astonishing about that?' he asked with irony. 'We can barely keep our hands off each other.'

'You…I…'

'You've fitted in as if you were made for the place—in fact there've been times, Chattie, when I've seen you walk around this house as if you own it, as if you *are* the lady of the house.'

'I haven't,' she denied huskily and looked appalled.

He smiled twistedly. 'Believe me, you have. And it's not only the house—I get the feeling the whole of Helena appeals to you very much.'

She knitted her fingers, then unknitted them. 'I…I…it does, but that's no reason to…to marry you.'

'How about this, then?' he said sardonically. 'Since it weighs so heavily with you, it would secure your sister's future.'

She could only stare at him open-mouthed.

'Tell me this…' he paused and watched her narrowly '…are we in agreement that forcing them to marry, Bridget and Mark, unless it's what they *both* want, is not the solution?'

She cleared her throat. 'Yes, but—'

'If you married me, Chattie, Bridget and her child would always have a home at Mount Helena, the child would be recognized as Mark's and she would be treated as part of the family.'

'It should be recognized as Mark's anyway,' she protested.

He shrugged. 'Naturally. But if Mark doesn't come

to the party, it's not going to be of much benefit to Bridget unless you're here at Mount Helena.'

'But, say Mark doesn't come to the party, how awkward will it be to have Bridget and his child living here?'

'They'll have to handle it as best they can but in point of fact I don't see Mark ever settling down here. And contrary to your view of me...' he paused and eyed her insolently '...I would never have consented to a Kinane simply being abandoned.'

Chattie flinched. 'I...I still...would need to think about this.'

'What's to think about?' He searched her eyes. 'This morning—was quite a revelation I would have thought.'

'What do you mean?'

He looked mocking. 'You know what I mean, Chattie. You admitted you wanted me as much as I want you. Has that changed over the last few hours?'

'This morning,' she said with an effort, 'we were discussing the next two weeks.'

He shrugged. 'Your sister is the one who's pushed us up a few gears.'

'Steve,' she said, and shivered suddenly, 'how can you want to marry me when you're...angry with me at the same time?'

His gaze clashed with hers. 'I'm sure that will pass.' He smiled but not with his eyes. 'I could even tell you what would make it pass rather—delightfully. But as a business proposition it would be entirely beneficial for both of us as well as Bridget, don't you think?'

The look in her grey eyes said it all—disbelief and growing anger plus something he couldn't quite identify. Hurt, perhaps? he wondered, but even if it was it didn't appear to have the power to deflect him from the course he was on. A course apparently becoming more and more set in concrete in his mind since he'd discovered how he'd been duped.

'It's not often one gets the opportunity to mix business with pleasure the way we could, Chattie,' he added musingly.

That did it. The explosion he was waiting for—had even hoped to provoke?—came.

She sprang up with her fists clenched and opened her mouth.

'Let me guess,' he murmured and got up himself. 'I'd be the last man on the planet you'd marry? You'd rather consort with a snake?'

Chattie closed her mouth, almost biting her tongue as he took the words out of her mouth.

'Don't you think you're kidding yourself?' he added softly but lethally as he came to stand right in front of her.

She took a distraught breath. 'No.'

'Well, I do.' He reached for her. 'This morning you told me it was rather lovely, to be in my arms. What can have changed?'

'You've changed,' she said bitterly.

'In some essentials, not at all,' he assured her dryly. 'For instance—' he drew her closer '—all the while I was rescuing the guys who came down in their chopper, I was thinking of this.'

Chattie's eyes widened in disbelief.

'I know.' He looked momentarily wry. 'To have images of undressing you slowly and finding out what bra you're wearing today mixed in with the coordination of a search and rescue came as a bit of a surprise to me too. What have *you* been thinking about in the interim?'

Chattie closed her eyes. You, your wife, what you had in mind for us—until Bridget wiped it all out, she thought.

'Chattie?'

She couldn't speak as all the old magic began to course through her as his breath fanned her cheek and his hands moved slowly on her. She opened her eyes to see that he was looking down at her through half-closed lids in a way that left no doubt he desired her even, perhaps, in anger.

And she was mesmerized by that dark, intimate gaze to the extent of picturing him undressing her slowly—and the pleasure it would bring her. It was, in fact, almost as if it were happening so that her nipples peaked and she grew warm with her own desire. She dropped her face onto his shoulder with a husky little sound, a mixture of yearning and frustration.

How could it happen, though? How could this powerful physical force still exist between them when they were in more mental discord than they'd ever been?

Then his mouth met hers, and, if she knew anything, it was that 'how?' or 'why?' didn't come into it—it was simply happening.

What broke them apart was a strangled gasp coming from the doorway. And the voicer of that gasp was Bridget. Who then tottered into the room to sink into a chair saying, 'If this is what it looks to be, it's the best news I've had for weeks.'

Steve didn't release Chattie but he said to Bridget, 'So you don't mind me proposing to your sister?'

'Proposing!' Bridget's beautiful violet eyes rimmed by thick, dark, completely natural lashes almost fell out on stalks. 'Oh, my stars! No, of course I don't. I was beginning to think Chattie was so darn choosey she might never—' She broke off but began again immediately. 'And then there's the way she's always lectured me about rushing into things but—no! If it's what she wants, of course I don't!'

Steve looked down into Chattie's stunned eyes. 'How say you, Miss Winslow, the elder?'

If anyone had ever been saved by the bell, Chattie was to think later, she was at that critical moment, although the irony of it was that the outcome was to be the same…

At the time, however, her bell came in the form of a visitor who strode up the front steps, calling, 'Anyone home?'

This time Steve did let Chattie go. 'In the lounge, Ryan,' he called back with resignation.

The sound of boots being discarded came, then socked, though heavy footfalls padded down the hall and a large young man strolled into the lounge. 'Good day, mate! Come to meet the housekeeper from heaven,' he announced. 'Holy smoke! You sly dog, Steve, me boy,' he added as his eyes fell on Chattie and he came to a stop. 'Thought the old man was exaggerating but for once in his life he was spot on!'

Steve said irritably, 'This is Ryan Winters, Chattie. You met his mother and father last night.'

Ryan stuck his hand out to Chattie. 'It's a pleasure to meet you, ma'am, a real pleasure.' They shook hands, then Ryan noticed Bridget.

It was a different Bridget from the one who had

climbed off the plane. She'd changed into jeans, a figure-hugging cyclamen jumper, her hair was tidy, and although she wore no make-up she looked exquisite.

So it came as no surprise to Chattie to see the shire chairman's son do a double take rather as his father had done.

He said, 'Bloody hell, Steve, no one told me you had a harem of housekeepers from heaven!'

'I don't,' Steve replied abruptly. 'Bridget is Chattie's sister. What can I do for you, Ryan? You surely didn't drive all this way just to check out my housekeeper?'

'It was an incentive, I cannot deny,' Ryan said genially, 'but the main thrust of my visit is that piece of spraying equipment you promised to lend Dad last night.'

Steve grimaced. 'Have you ever used one of them before?'

'Nope. Thought that was the object of the exercise—if we find it practical and easy to use, we'll invest in one of our own. You got a minute to give me a demo?'

'Yes, he has.' Chattie found her voice at last. 'Dinner won't be ready for an hour.' She glanced at her watch and looked surprised. 'At least an hour,' she added. 'So I'll have to get cracking. Bridget, you can come and give me a hand. Nice to meet you, Ryan!' And ignoring Steve's mockery-laden gaze, she swished out of the room.

Bridget followed her into the kitchen looking confused.

'You don't really have to help,' Chattie said. 'I want to talk to you. Like a cuppa?'

'Thanks, yes, but I don't mind helping. Chattie, what is going on?'

Chattie boiled the kettle and, while she waited for it, got some peas for Bridget to shell. 'Sit down,' she advised. 'You can do them at the table. And just let me do this…' She put some wood into the stove, made the tea and took a cup to Bridget. 'And this…'

Several trips to the cold room and dry goods store yielded the ingredients for her dinner—a rack of lamb, a container of frozen soup, flour, sugar and butter to make an apple pie.

Bridget watched her narrowly as she sipped her tea, then she started to shell peas with a thoughtful frown, as if mentally viewing her sister through quite new eyes.

But Chattie, as she worked on the rack of lamb, inserting cloves of garlic and adding sprigs of rosemary, felt herself soothed and capable of starting to think straight for the first time for what seemed like hours. She put the lamb in the oven, the soup in a saucepan and got the rolling-pin and a pastry board.

'So he's not so bad, Mark's brother?' Bridget said tentatively.

'He—no.'

'Have you really fallen in love with him?'

Chattie measured flour and butter into a bowl and started to rub the butter into the flour. 'We—do seem to have clicked,' she said cautiously, 'but it's all so new and unexpected…' She gestured with floury fingers.

Bridget smiled faintly. 'You've been swept off your feet?' she suggested.

Chattie looked rueful. 'If you mean it's a reverse case of the pot calling the kettle black, perhaps. Bridge—' her busy fingers stilled and she looked across at her sister '—everyone here seems to think that Mark has gone back to his ex-fiancée, who lives in Broome of all places.'

'That's only because he doesn't know,' Bridget replied intensely.

'Honey,' Chattie sighed, 'I hate to be the one to say this, but I think we have to take into account the possibility that Mark won't be best pleased with your news. And we have to think of an alternative for you.'

'What do you mean?' Bridget asked, her eyes filling with tears.

'I mean we can't force Mark to marry you although Steve has indicated that they would provide some support and Mark would be recognized as the baby's father.'

A look of terror came to Bridget's eyes. 'But I don't want to do this on my own, Chattie!'

'You'll never have to do that. I'll always be there—'

'But I won't be able to work and you can't stop working—what kind of support?'

'Monetary,' Chattie said.

Bridget shivered. 'That sounds so cold and—'

'It's better than nothing,' Chattie pointed out.

Bridget laid her head on the table and started to weep.

Chattie went to the sink and washed her hands, then came back and put her arm around Bridget's shoulders. 'Please don't,' she said quietly and looked across the kitchen with unseeing eyes for a long moment. Then, much as Steve had said to her earlier, she said, 'There is another way.'

'What's that?' Bridget hiccupped.

Chattie drew out a chair and sat down. 'The one reason that would stop me from marrying Steve is you,' she said carefully.

Bridget sat up and licked some tears from her lip. *'Why?'*

'Well, it would be the perfect solution in most respects. Steve has said you and the baby could have a proper home here whatever happens with Mark. We'd be together, you and I. But, much as this place appeals to me—'

'I thought it must have,' Bridget broke in breathlessly. 'The last time you rang I got the feeling you were loving every minute of it. That's another reason I decided to come up.'

'Yes. Well. The downside, though, is how much it would appeal to *you*. It is isolated—'

'Chattie,' Bridget said tragically, 'ever since I found out I was pregnant I've felt as if I'm in…Siberia. Nothing could be as isolated as that feeling.'

Chattie's eyes filled with compassion but she knew she had to soldier on. 'The other thing is, if Mark doesn't want to marry you—' She held up a hand. 'I know, you don't even want to contemplate that, but we *have* to. If he doesn't—how hard will it be for you to live here?'

Bridget put her hands on her stomach and said nothing for almost a minute, but several expressions chased through her eyes. Then she drew a deep breath. 'Even if he doesn't want it, to know his baby has a home and at least some part of its heritage would be such a load off my mind. Oh, it would be hard, I guess, but I would do it for my baby.'

CHAPTER NINE

IN THE event, Chattie had to stretch her dinner because the Cooks popped in on their way past just as Steve came back from demonstrating the spray equipment.

She'd already experienced the hospitality the outback was famous for—although it obviously didn't extend to Ryan Winters and she wondered why—but it came as no surprise to hear Steve invite them to stay for dinner. No surprise, but quite some relief.

Mind you, she pointed out to herself, it's only delaying the evil moment.

But at least it provided some relief and normality from the tension, however temporary.

Bridget was introduced and Lucy Cook was delighted to meet Chattie's sister—it turned out that Lucy was an avid follower of fashion and dying to hear of all the latest trends.

It also, Chattie realised rather darkly, gave Bridget the opportunity to sum up Steve discreetly and be impressed as the meal progressed leisurely, companionably and with lots of laughter as Ray and Steve traded stories about the fixes cattle could get themselves into.

In fact she could see her sister relaxing visibly beneath the civilized aura of the evening—was she deciding that Mount Helena was not quite as isolated as she'd suspected and might even be a more enjoyable place to live than she'd thought? Chattie wondered.

But like all good things it came to an end. Bridget

helped her to clear up, then yawned hugely, so Chattie sent her to bed in the guest room next door to her own bedroom.

She was giving Rich a last walk in the garden when Steve found her. Rich had taken his time about bestowing his approval on Steve Kinane but he now walked up to him for a pat, wagging his tail, causing Chattie to wonder if it was some kind of an omen.

It was a crisp, clear night with a pale sliver of new moon, but the stars were huge and a lemon ironbark bush was scenting the dewy air.

'Quite a night,' he said.

'It's lovely,' Chattie replied, but pulled her jumper more closely around her.

'Quite a day, come to that. Do you often get these premonitions?'

She grimaced. 'No. Thank heavens.'

'Are we—talking to each other or not?'

She glanced at him. He'd leant his shoulders against the trunk of the ironbark, shoved his hands in his pockets and was regarding her thoughtfully. Throughout dinner he'd been perfectly normal towards her except for a couple of occasions when she'd discovered his dark eyes resting on her enigmatically.

'Steve…' she hesitated '…when did you plan to tell me about your ex-wife?'

'Right now, as a matter of fact—I had no doubt you'd already heard of her. I happened to overhear Merlene about to embark on that bit of gossip a couple of nights ago.'

Chattie frowned and remembered when she was making egg and caviare canapés. 'So that's why you were in a bad mood! I did wonder.'

'One of the reasons.'

'But—'

'Chattie, there is only one version of it you need to hear and that's mine,' he interrupted. 'As a matter of interest, who else has taken it upon themselves to enlighten you about Nadine?'

Chattie absolved Merlene, explained about Joan Jackson finding her in the music room and finding the wedding photo, but at the last moment decided to hold her peace about Harriet's two-bit worth. She finished by saying, 'I believe she was not suited to this kind of life.'

'No. She wasn't.'

'I can't help wondering if it's left you rather battle-scarred,' she said slowly.

'In what way?' He raised an eyebrow at her.

'Well, blackmailing me into a marriage of convenience could be a symptom of it, for example.'

'It wouldn't only be that, as you very well know.'

She shivered.

'Nor am I still in love with Nadine, I got over it years ago and she's remarried but, yes,' he said, 'I did swear that if I ever married again, I'd be a whole lot more practical about it. I would have thought that might appeal to you because you're such a practical person yourself.' He raised an eyebrow at her.

How to tell a man you were harbouring a secret little hope that he would fall madly, passionately and quite impractically in love with you? Chattie wondered, but couldn't find the answer so she said nothing.

'Besides which,' he went on after a long moment, 'I'm tired of being a bachelor. I'd like to have my own kids rather than using Brett as a surrogate son.

I'd like to have someone to make plans with, someone whose company I enjoy and who enjoys this place, someone who'll keep me from becoming a dried-up, boring old cattle-man. You.'

Chattie felt her heart move in her breast because he'd spoken quietly but she got the feeling he meant every word and she couldn't help being curiously moved.

'And that's all without what we do to each other physically.' He straightened and she tensed but he made no move towards her. 'Would it be so inconceivable?' he asked.

Not at all, if I didn't suspect you're still angry with me, might never fully trust me or—could just say three little words—I love you, it ran through her mind.

Her next thought was that if it was so important for her to hear those three words, could she any longer doubt that she'd fallen in love with him?

'Steve—' She broke off.

He surprised her. 'Sleep on it,' he said, and this time he did move towards her, but only to take her face in his hands and add barely audibly, 'I think you'd make a wonderful wife, Chattie Winslow.'

He released her after a long, shared and searching glance, and walked away.

They were alone at breakfast the next morning.

'Morning—how is Bridget?' were his first words to her as he sat down to bacon and eggs.

'Dead to the world so I'll let her sleep in,' Chattie replied.

He studied her in a pair of caramel cord trousers and a pink crinkly cotton blouse with a drawstring neckline as she brought the toast. For some reason her hair was severely tamed into a tight-looking knot and there were faint blue shadows beneath her eyes as if she hadn't slept too well.

He waited for her to sit down before he said simply, 'So?'

Chattie reached for the butter. 'Thank you, the answer is yes.'

Their gazes clashed and for a moment Chattie was convinced she was right about something that had popped into her head during a long and difficult night. That this was some kind of a test, this proposal of marriage from Steve Kinane, a test she would fail if she agreed to marry him…

He went to say something but appeared to change his mind and said instead as he got up, 'Stay there.' And left the kitchen.

When he came back he had a small, old, leather-bound box in his hand. He flicked it open and put it beside her plate.

Chattie's eyes widened—it was an engagement ring. Obviously not new, it was nevertheless quite lovely, an oval ruby surrounded by tiny diamonds to make a flower shape and set on a gold band.

'But…whose…what…?' She looked up bewilderedly.

'It was my mother's.'

'Didn't…I mean your first wife, didn't she—?'

'No. My mother was still alive then,' he said, and, putting his hand over hers, drew her to her feet. 'This may not be the most romantic setting,' he added as he took the ring from the box and slid it on her finger, 'but my mother would have approved of you very much.'

It was all so unexpected, Chattie raised her grey eyes to his and they were deeply bewildered.

How had he managed to bridge the chasm that existed between them? A chasm caused by her deceiving him over Bridget and resulting in this proposal being made in the form of blackmail. Or rather, she thought, why was he doing it this way now? Had the cynicism he'd displayed yesterday dried up or was she being lured into a false sense of security?

'It's normal to kiss the bride-to-be in this situation,' he said softly and traced the outline of her mouth. 'Would it be permissible?'

She swallowed.

'Do you like the ring?'

'It's lovely.' She looked down at it on her finger. 'Uh—thank you.'

'My pleasure.' He enfolded the slim length of her against him. 'Mmm…you smell nice.'

She looked surprised. 'Must be my shampoo, I haven't used any perfume.'

'Might just be the essential you but, talking of shampoo, what have you done to your poor hair this morning?'

'I decided to look practical.'

Their gazes caught and his eyes told her he'd registered her attempt at a shot against him, but he was too clever for her. He countered it by fiddling with the bobbles restraining her hair until he got it free in all its fair, curly splendour.

'There, that's how I like it,' he murmured. 'Wayward and gorgeous, like the rest of you. In fact so much so I can no longer restrain myself from doing this.'

He put his arms around her again and lowered his mouth to hers.

Chattie thought of resisting but he foiled that too as his hands moved on her body to cup her breasts and trace the outline of her hips, then slide along the satiny skin of her upper arms—and she was lost.

Her nipples started to direct a stream of sensuous traffic throughout her slim figure, not only beneath the feel of his hands on her, but also the hard, warm feel of his body against hers. All sorts of secret areas of her body clamoured for his attentions and her breathing grew ragged as she felt herself budding and flowering like a thirsty garden crying out to be nurtured by Steve Kinane and Steve Kinane alone.

Then he untied the drawstring of her blouse and pulled it apart to reveal a hyacinth-blue bra trimmed with white and green flowers.

'It gets better and better,' he said against the corner of her mouth, and started to kiss the soft hollows at the base of her throat.

Chattie felt herself melting against him and she made a husky little sound of sheer need.

'Mmm, I'm rather a fan of it myself.' He pushed the shoulders of her blouse further down, then cupped her hips to him as he kissed, tasted and literally set her on fire as his mouth moved down towards her breasts.

From somewhere it came to Chattie that they were on a course they wouldn't be able to deflect themselves from very soon, unless she made a supreme effort.

'Maybe you shouldn't go there,' she whispered.

He raised his head and there was a wicked little glint in his eyes. 'No?'

'No. They seem to have a mind of their own as it is, but with your encouragement...' She trailed off.

'I like the sound of that.'

'All the same, perhaps this isn't the time or the place.'

'There are six bedrooms in this house,' he reminded her.

'I meant,' she said, barely audibly because it was difficult enough to talk, let alone going to be incredibly difficult to disengage from Steve Kinane now, 'I think we should wait until we're married.'

Surprise, or something, held him silent for a beat. Until he said. 'The sooner the better, then.'

And Merlene's motor bike made itself heard approaching.

He grimaced. 'Saved by the bell maybe. Because I get the feeling wherever we ''go'' in this manner could be problematic for us now.'

She licked her lips and tried to calm her breathing as well as all the lovely sensations running through her while he tied up her blouse. Then she realized he was watching her intently and expecting some kind of a response, some confirmation that they were in this together and there was no way—much as some instinct told her she might regret it—she could deny him that confirmation.

'Yes.'

Something flickered in his eyes and he took her hand and turned her towards the back door as Merlene strode in.

'Morning, boss! Morning, Chattie! Just went down to get the milk. Tell you what, it's a pleasure to have the place to ourselves, well, more…or…less,' Merlene wound down with a frown as she took in the picture Steve and Chattie made, only to demand then, 'Is this what I think it is?'

'Depends,' Steve replied. 'We're getting married.'

'I knew that!'

'How?' Chattie asked incredulously.

'What I mean to say is,' Merlene amended herself, 'I knew he'd do things by the book. Well, well, well! I don't think I could have done better for you if I'd chosen her myself.'

'Thank you,' Steve said gravely.

'OK! When? And where?'

'Here, of course—' He stopped. 'Actually, we haven't discussed that yet, Merlene.' He looked humorous.

'If the things I've been hearing are true,' Merlene said, 'the sooner you do, the better.'

Chattie blushed, Steve looked briefly irritated, then shrugged. 'The bush telegraph at its worst.'

'You shouldn't go around kissing her in public, then,' Merlene retorted, but came up to Chattie and shook her hand. 'You done good, kid. I have to tell you even Slim would approve and there's a hard man to please.'

Steve had to leave shortly after that but he promised he'd be back for lunch and had the afternoon free so they could make some plans.

'One thing,' he said just before he departed. 'What does Bridget know about all this?'

'She has no idea I'm—' She stopped abruptly as she wondered how to phrase it. Doing it all for her—was what she'd been about to say. But even if she was being pressured into marrying Steve, was that completely true?

'Chattie?'

She looked up at him at last. 'She doesn't know what precipitated it,' she said carefully.

'I see. Doesn't know that you're going to be a martyr on her behalf?' he suggested softly.

She stared into his dark eyes. 'I didn't say that.'

'No. But something's bothering you,' he countered. 'How many times do I have to kiss you and hold you to get you to believe—?'

'Don't say any more, Steve,' she advised. 'You've made that point and I accept it. I can't help feeling a little shell-shocked, though.' She gestured helplessly. 'We've only known each other for little more than a week.'

'Interesting you should make that point. Nadine and I knew each other for nine months before we got married.'

Chattie blinked. 'That long? So why…?'

'Why didn't it last?' he drawled. 'We didn't have enough in common. Why don't you reflect on that until I get back?' He turned to go but turned back. 'And this.' He pulled her into his arms and kissed her until she was breathless. Then he left without another word.

'So you're going to do it?'

Chattie had brought a breakfast tray for Bridget and her sister was sitting propped up in bed with the tray on her knees. She had immediately noticed the engagement ring on Chattie's left hand.

'Yes.' Chattie sat down in an armchair with the coffee she'd brought for herself, and added honestly, 'I don't know if I'm on my head or my heels.'

'That's just how I felt with Mark,' Bridget said reminiscently and began to look tearful, but she battled it resolutely and started to eat her boiled egg. 'Isn't it funny, though,' she said, 'that the two people I love most should have such differing views of Steve Kinane?'

Do we? Chattie wondered. I'm not so sure...

'Steve explained about the problems he and Mark have, Bridge,' she said, however. And she went on to tell Bridget what Steve had said.

'I guess that makes sense.' Bridget pushed her egg away and reached for her coffee. 'You know what he'd really like to do?'

'Mark? Something artistic?' Chattie hazarded.

Bridget shook her head. 'Apparently he's very good with horses.'

Chattie grimaced. 'Must run in the family, so is Steve. Go on.'

'Well, he'd love to be a racehorse trainer.'

'Why doesn't he?' Chattie asked slowly.

'I think it only came to him recently that the artistic side he inherited from his mother wasn't strong enough for any career in it. And, from what you've told me, I can't help wondering if he felt he would be letting his mother down somehow if he didn't go that way.'

'Perhaps,' Chattie conceded.

'It would be enough to make you a bit mixed-up, wouldn't it?' Bridget said.

'Yes.' Chattie drained her coffee.

'Still and all…' Bridget stretched '…that's enough of Mark. I've got to stop thinking about it, somehow. I will,' she assured Chattie.

Chattie got up. 'Have a shower and get dressed and I'll show you around a bit more.' But as she left the room she couldn't help wondering if Bridget might be growing up at last, and quite fast.

Steve didn't make it for lunch—Bill delivered the message to the homestead, adding that Chattie's presence was required at the bunkhouse at two o'clock.

'What for?' Chattie asked him.

He shrugged. 'Search me, I'm only the messenger. But the boss said wear jeans and boots if you've got any.'

Chattie frowned. 'A cross-country hike?'

'Dunno.'

At two o'clock Chattie and Bridget presented themselves at the bunkhouse, to find Harriet in attendance.

'You must be Chattie's sister,' Harriet said and shook Bridget's hand. 'I'm Mark and Steve's cousin—which will make me your baby's second cousin or something like that.'

Chattie took an unexpected breath, not sure whether to be angry or relieved that the news had been broken so summarily.

But Harriet turned to her with an engaging grin. 'And I guess we'll be cousins-in-law. Congratulations! Just don't forget what I told you,' she added in an undertone. 'OK, Steve's got plans for you and I've got plans for Bridget.'

Chattie opened her mouth but Steve came round the corner of the bunkhouse leading two saddled horses.

Half an hour later, Chattie was mounted on one of the horses, alongside Steve mounted on the other and connected by a leading rein. Bridget and Harriet had stayed to witness the initiation lesson Chattie had received—with some hilarity—then Harriet had shepherded Bridget towards her Range Rover.

'I don't know,' Chattie started to say anxiously.

'It'll be all right,' Steve assured her quietly. 'Harriet has pledged to be on her best behaviour. She's taking her home with her for coffee and a chat, that's all. Harriet's as bad as Lucy Cook when it comes to fashion and I thought the sooner we get all the awkwardness out of the way, the better it will be for Bridget.'

'Harriet can be staggeringly undiplomatic, though,' Chattie pointed out.

'Harriet will do exactly as I told her.' He folded his arms and regarded her gravely. 'Did you not once tell me, only yesterday as it happens, that you would love to ride a horse?'

'Well, yes, but—'

'Good. She's yours.' He indicated the chestnut one of the two horses.

Chattie's mouth fell open.

'She's a four-year-old mare, a stock horse with a lovely nature, and I'd already decided to turn her into a hack. Shall we give it a try?'

As a recipe for having the wind taken completely out of one's sails, being given your own horse and then to receive a riding lesson on it was unparalleled Chattie discovered.

Hard as she tried to bear in mind Steve's autocratic ways, she couldn't hold onto her resentment. Nor could she stifle the thought that he was right, the sooner the awkwardness of it all was banished, the better for, not only Bridget, but also all concerned. Finally, the pleasure in what she was doing took over completely.

'You could be a natural,' he told her as she gained the confidence to break into a slow canter. 'Don't forget the angle to have your feet in the stirrups—heels down, toes up.'

'Why is that?'

'Should you ever have to get off in hurry, you can just slip your feet out. Shall we have a bit of a break?' He indicated a patch of gum-trees beside a dam.

She nodded, and when they dismounted they gave the horses a drink and he showed her how to tie them to trees on a long rein so they could crop the grass.

'What's her name?' she asked as she stroked the mare's nose.

'Would you believe Cathy Freeman?'

Chattie looked amused. 'That's an odd name for a stock horse!'

'I know, but Bill names all the stock horse foals and he uses sportsmen and women. We have a Tiger Woods, a Pete Sampras and a Venus Williams.'

Chattie laughed delightedly, and when Steve sank down onto the grass she followed suit. 'Could we bring Rich along the next time we do this?'

'Sure. Rich is another one to take to this place almost as if he was born to it. Chattie, tell me about your parents?'

She pulled a stalk of grass, chewed it and looked at him questioningly.

'I just wondered what there might be in your background to account for...' he spread an arm '...the way you could almost have been born to this.'

A spark of interest lit her grey eyes. 'You could be right. My father was a stock and station agent. He said it was the next best thing to owning a station, which he couldn't afford. We lived in Toowoomba on what was really a hobby farm but, when they died, had to move to Brisbane to my mother's sister.'

'No other relations? Is she still alive?'

'No other relations and she passed away a year ago.'

'I see,' he said slowly. 'What about friends?'

'Oh, I've got plenty of those—is this conversation leading somewhere, Mr Kinane?' she asked with a glint of humour.

'Yep. Where to hold the wedding.'

Chattie sobered.

'Still shell-socked?' he queried.

She glanced across at him. He wore his usual jeans and bush shirt and as he lazily waved away some bush flies she was literally assaulted by everything that was fine, strong but also determined about him. A hard man to cross, it popped into her mind, a hard man to say no to...

She plucked another stalk of grass and was dismayed to find that her hand was trembling beneath all the things Steve Kinane did to her. I'll be a basket case shortly, it occurred to her, if I go on wanting him yet resenting him at times, like this.

'I have given it some thought,' she said cautiously. 'For Bridget's sake, something low key would be best.'

'Why?'

The way he said it told her she was in for a fight, and she took a deep breath. 'She's the one who was hoping to be married. A big wedding couldn't help but—well, make her think of what might have been for *her*.'

'Your devotion to your sister is commendable, Chattie, but there has to be a limit. No, listen to me,' he said quietly as she made a sudden move, and he put a hand over hers. 'There's going to be enormous curiosity in the district about this marriage as it is. For your sake, the best way to deal with it is not to be low-key or—hole-in-the-corner.'

'But—'

'I'm not,' he overrode her, 'suggesting anything flamboyant or over-the-top. But the ceremony and reception here at Helena should satisfy the district and, even more importantly—if we're going to do this, it would give me the reassurance that it's not all going to be hard labour for you.'

Their eyes met.

'We could fly in as many of your friends as you'd like,' he added. 'You could be the bride—of your choice.'

Chattie fixed her gaze on Cathy Freeman for a long moment, and commanded herself to think straight. What good would it do for any of them if she was giving off 'hard labour' vibes?

'OK,' she said. 'But I'll have to go back to Brisbane to wind up my—our lives there, first.'

'Your job?' he queried.

'I have two months' untaken leave up my sleeve,' she said slowly. 'I worked on preparation programs right through the last Christmas holidays, so I can use that as notice.' She gestured. 'Not how I would like to do it, but the best I can come up with.'

'Why don't we combine that trip to Brisbane with some shopping?' he suggested. 'We could fly down.'

'Bridget,' Chattie began.

'Bridget could come with us, if she's game to fly again.'

Chattie subsided. Then she asked, 'When—should we do it? Get married, I mean?'

'How about—three weeks from today?'

'Make it four and you've got a deal,' she said with another glint of humour.

He raised a wry eyebrow. 'Think we can last out that long?'

A tinge of pink entered her cheeks. 'We'll have to,' she said, however. 'I always wanted to design and make my own wedding dress, and, if we're going to satisfy the district and come up with a suitable wedding for them, and me, I'll need a month.' She got up and added gently, 'That's my last offer, incidentally, but you won't regret it.'

He rose to his feet. 'Talk about being caught by the short and curlies—my apologies—'

But Chattie started to laugh, she just couldn't help—as he looked extremely rueful.

He laughed with her. Then he helped her back on her horse, and they rode home with Chattie, mysteriously, feeling better than she had for a while.

CHAPTER TEN

MYSTERIOUSLY, also, Bridget had enjoyed her session with Harriet, Chattie discovered. Had Steve put the fear of God into his wayward cousin? Chattie wondered.

'She treated me as if I was one of the family,' Bridget said, wonderingly. 'I really thought they'd all hate me. And she gave me some tips about being pregnant, what to expect and so on. Apparently, the middle three months are best. Harriet got over all her morning sickness by then and she glowed!'

'That is good news!' Chattie responded wryly. 'Have you felt sick at all today?'

'Not really. Just a bit queasy after breakfast.'

'OK—I need to take a shower. Could you peel some potatoes for me?'

'Sure! What's for dinner?'

'Pork chops.'

'Would you like me to make that potato casserole with onions and tomatoes?'

'You're a honey, yes, please!' And Chattie closed herself into her bedroom to shower and change for dinner—and to think about the forthcoming expedition to Brisbane.

In the event, it wasn't Steve who took her to Brisbane, it was Joan Jackson.

While Chattie was showering she rang in to say that

John had insisted she visit a specialist about her migraines, and he was flying her down the next morning and leaving her there for a couple of days, so was there anything they needed from the Big Smoke?

Steve took the call, hesitated then asked her if he could call her back. And he went on to first find Bridget, then Chattie.

As he knocked then opened her bedroom door her head and arms emerged through the neckline and sleeves of a slate-blue dress that floated around her before subsiding against her figure.

'Sorry.' He leant back against the door.

'That's OK. I'm decent now,' she answered, although she looked faintly flustered. 'What can I do you for?'

He told her about Joan Jackson's call, and finished by saying, 'The thing is, I wondered if you'd like to go down with Joan rather than me.'

Chattie's lips parted. 'Why?'

'Because there's rain on the way, according to the weather forecast I've just heard, and there's a mob of cattle I'm particularly keen to muster before it gets here. The more hands I can muster, the better.'

Chattie smiled and was just about to comment on the joys of being a cattleman's wife, but something stopped her. 'Uh, well, but what about Bridget?'

'Nothing would induce Bridget to set foot on a light plane at the moment.'

'You've already checked with her?' Chattie looked surprised.

'Yep. I also rang Harriet and she'd be happy to have Bridget stay with her while you're away.'

'How on earth did you get Harriet to be

so…so…compliant and helpful?' she couldn't help asking.

His lips twisted. 'I told her what you told me—this has happened and we need to make the best of it rather than indulge in an orgy of recriminations. But, it so happens, Harriet is rather taken with your sister.'

'Most people are,' Chattie commented.

'Point taken.' Their gazes caught and held and he straightened and came towards her. 'Are you happy to go with Joan, then? She'd probably be a lot more helpful than I would be with the wedding preparations. She's married three daughters off.'

'All right,' Chattie said slowly.

'You don't sound convinced.'

'The speed with which you organize things takes my breath away at times, that's all.' She half smiled.

He hesitated, then, 'Sorry, but anyway, shouldn't most of the preparations be a surprise for the groom?'

'Traditionally, I guess so.'

'Why don't we opt for all tradition, then?' He suggested. 'After all, we're being very traditional in one area.'

She looked up at him with a question in her eyes, but comprehension came to them as his dark gaze slipped down her figure.

She stirred and drew an unsteady breath. Her dress was loose but its silky material clung to her breasts and she felt very much on display to Steve Kinane with all the attendant sensations that brought. And she was drawn, in her mind, to a vision of them preparing to make love. Of them kissing and discarding their clothes with sensual serenity as they gloried in each other's bodies.

It came to her that to be unclothed against the strong, hard planes of his body and to have his hands explore her nakedness might draw more from her than serenity—it might be a soul-liberating experience at the same time…

She swallowed and wiped the dew of sweat from her brow with the back of her hand as she wondered if he was as affected as she was.

Then, as he placed his hands on her shoulders and drew her into his arms, knew that he was. But he only kissed the top of her head—and released her.

'I think this might be a no-go zone—at this point in time, Chattie,' he said with a glint of humour in his eyes, but a tell-tale nerve beating in his jaw.

She smiled shakily. 'I think you could be right.'

'Should we—adjourn to dinner, then?'

'Definitely!'

Joan Jackson was almost as excited as if she were marrying a daughter off again.

By the time she and Chattie were ensconced in adjoining rooms at a luxury hotel the next day, she'd given Chattie and Steve her blessing. She'd told Chattie that at their first meeting she'd harboured the thought that Chattie was exactly what Steve needed. And, on Chattie venturing to say that some people might question the suddenness of it, she'd advised her that she and John Jackson had known within days of meeting that they were made for each other.

Then Chattie discovered that Joan was a mine of information on how to organize a wedding and she'd thought to bring along her diaries from the years of her daughter's weddings. Florists, bridal boutiques, printers, cake makers, caterers prepared to go up country and likewise hairdressers, plus a whole lot more came out of Joan's diaries.

Chattie attempted to stem the flow somewhat by telling Joan she meant to make her own dress and her own wedding cake, that she didn't need caterers or a hairdresser, and she wasn't planning on having bridesmaids.

Joan eventually backed down on the dress, the cake and the hairdresser, but stood quite firm on all the rest.

Until Chattie said with dawning suspicion in her eyes, 'Has Steve been laying down the law to you?'

Joan grimaced. 'In a way. He told me to make sure you didn't take too much upon yourself, and to spare no expense so that it will be a lovely, memorable occasion! Now, what more could you ask from a man?'

Chattie had to smile, although a shade ruefully. What indeed? Unless you resented being manipulated?

'And, of course, you must have your sister as a bridesmaid and I *know* Harriet would love to be the matron of honour.'

Three days later they flew back laden down with parcels.

Apart from her appointment with the specialist, Joan and Chattie had spent all their time together. As a shopper, Joan had proven to be intuitive with a keen eye for value and quality, and a terror when it came to laying down the law to caterers and florists, and deadlines to printers of wedding invitations.

She'd also been helpful with the winding up of Chattie's and Bridget's lives in Brisbane. All their belongings had been packed up to be trucked to Mount

Helena; the lease on their rented cottage renegotiated to a new tenant; their car placed with a car yard for sale. And Chattie had visited her TAFE college and broken the news of her marriage and defection.

The one thing she'd stopped short of doing was contacting any of her friends. She'd run out of time but, not only that, as she dismantled her previous life and prepared for an unexpected wedding she was often attacked by disbelief. Mostly she could stifle it, sometimes not and the thought of getting in touch with friends was one of those times.

It was late afternoon as Chattie disembarked at Mount Helena and Joan stayed aboard for the last leg of the flight. 'We done well!' she said to Chattie as she kissed her goodbye.

'Thanks to you!' Chattie responded warmly. 'I'll let you know when the dress is ready—perhaps John will fly you over for a sneak preview?'

It was John himself who answered, 'If I know a thing or two, Chattie, between now and the wedding, we'll be doing a lot of buzzing backwards and forwards. Bye now!'

Merlene came to meet the plane, not Steve and Bridget as Chattie had expected, and she brought the news that they'd had a bit of drama with the muster, one of the ringers had fallen off his horse and broken some ribs, and Steve was staying with him until they could helicopter him out.

'But he's OK himself?' Chattie asked.

'Yep. And your sister's fine, so is Rich. Glory be,' Merlene remarked as they loaded parcel after parcel into the back of the Range Rover. 'You leave anything back in the shops in Brissie, kid?'

Chattie laughed. 'I've just spent three days with the most determined shopper I've ever met in my life! She claims it comes from only being let loose twice a year—I wonder if I'll end up the same?'

'Could do! Can't say I go for it much myself,' Merlene opined, but she brought a pot of tea to Chattie's bedroom and sat down to go through all Chattie's purchases with keen interest.

'Where are they, by the way? Bridget and Rich?' Chattie asked.

'Still down at the Barlow abode—have those two ever clicked, which is a good thing for your sister in her condition! And of course you know what Brett thinks of Rich. How about we invite the Barlows up for dinner? You up to it?'

'Of course. But will Steve and Jack—?'

'Should be by then. I'll give Harriet a bell.'

Left on her own in the colourful chaos of her bedroom, Chattie sank down onto the bed and suddenly experienced one of those moments of disbelief, only it turned out to be much more than a niggle.

I can't believe this is happening to me, she thought, and suddenly felt as if she were suffocating. It's like being on a runaway train headed towards marriage to a man who wants me but hasn't fallen in love with me and I don't know if I can do it...

Do what? she asked herself.

'Stand the way I'm being railroaded into this,' she said aloud. 'Stand the thought of a marriage of convenience when I want to be loved. When I don't want the dark side of Steve Kinane to come between us but I know it's there.'

To her horror, she discovered tears rolling down her cheeks as she felt more shaky, emotional and scared than she'd ever felt in her life. And prey to a powerful instinct simply to run away.

Think of Bridget, she commanded herself. If nothing else, he has gone out of his way to make things as easy as possible for her. Hold onto that, Chattie, you must!

Steve came home just as Harriet, Bridget, Brett and Rich arrived at the homestead, and he had to wait his turn to greet her. Jack was on his way, having stopped to shower and change.

'Remember me?' he queried softly as he took her in his arms.

'The man who sent me to Brisbane?' she replied and attempted a teasing little smile. 'I think so.'

'What's wrong?' His gaze narrowed.

'Nothing! It's been a big three days, that's all.'

'Then why this bun fight?'

'It—was Merlene's idea. Plus—' she groped desperately for more humour '—you forgot to warn me about how stiff a novice horse rider would get.'

He looked wry. 'Bad?'

'My legs are killing me.'

'I know exactly how to help. A good massage works wonders.'

The thought of him massaging her thighs went straight to Chattie's head and she turned pink and trembled in his arms.

'That's better,' he murmured. 'I thought you'd gone away from me.'

'And if I had?' she asked barely audibly.

'I would not approve of that at all.' He stared down

into her eyes, and something incredibly determined glinted in his own.

But before Chattie could respond Harriet said teasingly, 'Now, enough of that, you two love birds, there are children present!'

They broke apart as everyone laughed.

It was a cheerful meal during which the wedding preparations were discussed. Cheerful, that was, apart from Bridget, who got quieter and quieter, causing Chattie to wonder helplessly how she was going to get her sister through it all.

But it broke up fairly early, the Barlows went home and she and Bridget were doing the dishes when another vehicle drove up to the garden gate.

'Who on earth could that be?' Chattie wondered aloud as she heard Steve walk out onto the veranda.

'I don't know about isolated, there seem to be an awful lot of comings and goings out here,' Bridget said ruefully and stiffened as a voice greeted Steve.

Chattie frowned and looked a question at her.

Mark! Bridget mouthed and moved convulsively.

But Chattie put a warning hand on her arm, then gestured to her sister to follow her into the passage where they could hear clearly.

'This is a surprise, Mark!' Steve said. 'Where the hell have you been?'

'Sorting out my life,' Mark Kinane replied, 'as you've so often recommended I do, big bro. Not that you're likely to approve of what I've done, but will you please just listen?'

There was a pause, then Steve said dryly, 'Go ahead.'

What came next was the sound of chairs being scraped back as the two men sat down.

Then Mark's voice came again. 'I've got a job. The one thing I really want to do is train racehorses so I applied to a Sydney trainer and he's taken me on for six months as his assistant. A house goes with the position. You know him, Brian Matthews, he's got a good record of training winners, and a lot that he could pass on. Then, in six months, I hope to be able to establish my own stables.'

'What could I object to about that?' Steve asked. 'I think you'd make a damn fine trainer and I'd be more than happy to give you some horses.'

'Thanks. It's not that, though, it's the reason behind it, the reason that made me see I had to stop drifting and do something with my life. The thing is, I'm getting married.'

Bridget froze.

'I know you'll say I'm too young,' Mark continued, 'we're too young and all that garbage, but I know she's the one for me and I won't be talked out of it. I just—can't live without her, I want a family with her and the hardest thing I've done lately is be away from her. But I thought I had to tell you this in person. I'm driving down to see her first thing tomorrow.'

'Who is she?'

'No one you know.'

'She has a name, I presume.'

'Bridget Winslow, and she's the loveliest girl in the world.'

Chattie took her hand off Bridget's arm and made a little shooing gesture. Her sister flew down the passage and out onto the veranda. Chattie followed, although more sedately, but in time to see Mark Kinane turn, look absolutely stunned, then rise in time to catch Bridget in his arms.

'Bridge, oh, Bridge, sweetheart! What are you doing here?'

'No one would believe me, but I knew you loved me as much as I love you, Mark, and I just knew you'd come back to me!'

'A double wedding?' Steve said.

Chattie was standing on the front veranda, staring out over the starlight silvered garden and paddocks. Both Mark and Bridget had just retired after a couple of hours of such joy, it had been hard not to be affected. And she had been affected, deeply affected for Bridget's sake. However immature and impetuous they might be, you couldn't doubt that Mark Kinane was deeply in love with her sister and she with him.

The discovery that Bridget was pregnant had drawn an awed response from Steve's brother, and together they'd barely been able to stop themselves speculating on which occasion they'd made love that it had happened.

But it was also outside Chattie's power to stop herself from being negatively affected, as she'd identified the difference between Bridget's situation and her own. The difference mutual love made as opposed to physical desire and a business arrangement, in other words.

She turned at last to find Steve standing right behind her. 'No, no double wedding. I can't do it, Steve.'

She thought his breath rasped in his throat and she tensed visibly.

'Why not?' he asked grimly.

'There is no reason for me to marry you now.'

'No *reason*?' he growled. 'It was never only Bridget and you damn well know it, Chattie.'

'It *was* Bridget—at least, she was the lever you used. Well,' she said bitterly, 'that lever has disappeared and what's left? A business arrangement, practicality, how well I'm suited to Mount Helena, how good I'd be for the place and you—but have you ever once stopped to wonder how well you and Mount Helena are suited to *me*?'

'If I had you in my arms,' he taunted, 'there would be no question of how well we suit each other.'

'Steve, I'm going on twenty-three and a virgin,' she said with tears slipping down her cheeks. 'That's fairly remarkable in this day and age, but I made a conscious decision that sex should be very special and reserved for a very special relationship: marriage. OK, I had to make some adjustments when I was desperate about Bridget, but now I don't because "practical" and "business arrangements" don't fall into that category.'

He was silent for an age. Silent, frowning and as watchful as a hawk. Until she took a hankie from her pocket to blow her nose, and went to turn away. Then he put a hand on her shoulder.

'So you really don't want to marry me, Chattie?'

'No, Steve, I don't. Not like this. I may have a down-to-earth side, but I'm not so firmly planted in the ground that I don't know the difference between real joy in a man and a woman—which is what I would need—and what you're offering me.'

'That's the best news I've heard for a while.'

Chattie's heart started to beat like a muffled drum as all hope slipped away. Then she swallowed. 'So, it's all sorted,' she said huskily. 'I may even get back to Brisbane in time to get my job back and stop them selling my car.'

'No, it's not all sorted,' he said and scanned her pale, strained face in the starlight. 'Because I've been trying to kid myself that I haven't fallen madly in love with you, Chattie, since the day we met.'

Her lips parted. 'You...have?'

'Yes.' He put his fingertips lightly on her cheek, then shoved his hands in his pocket as if he was afraid to touch her again. 'You see, I not only swore to be more practical about marriage if I did it again, but I swore never to fall in love again.'

'She hurt you that badly?' Chattie whispered.

'I thought so at the time. Now I know it was nothing compared to having to watch you walk away from me. My problem was, Nadine deceived me. She didn't want me, she wanted my money. She thought she could separate me from Helena and it drove her crazy when she couldn't. She had affairs to make me jealous, she...' He stopped and shrugged. 'I guess I thought I'd become an iron man emotionally.'

'And it didn't help when you discovered I'd deceived you too?' Chattie said on a breath.

'No, it didn't, although it probably couldn't have been in a better cause. If the way you take care of your sister is the way you would take care of anyone you love, Chattie, I couldn't admire you more. But, not thinking too rationally, I have to admit, it raised— I couldn't help thinking, Here I go again! In love with a woman who wants something from me, not just *me*.'

'Oh, Steve.' Her eyes were wet again. 'I couldn't help wondering if it was some kind of a test.'

'I know, crazy, wasn't it? Insane, even, because I would have married you come hell or high water, Chattie.' He closed his eyes briefly.

'And been suspicious and angry underneath at the same time,' she murmured. 'I knew that.' She paused and took a deep breath. 'May I ask you something?'

He nodded.

'Will you marry me, Steve?'

He moved abruptly. 'It's that—it is that special?' he queried unevenly.

'It's that special, now,' she agreed with no more tears slipping down her cheeks, with stars in her eyes instead. 'Because I too have been trying to pretend that I haven't fallen madly in love with you ever since we met.'

His taut, hawk-like stance relaxed at last. 'My darling Chattie,' he murmured and pulled her into his arms, 'if only you knew what a…damn roundabout I've been on since you walked into my life. How I've hated myself lately for even hoping I was hurting you because at least that would mean you felt the way I did or something of it.'

'I did, I do! And I've been on the same roundabout,' she confessed. 'Not that I wanted to hurt you, but sometimes I couldn't help hating you and—' She broke off and shivered.

'Never again.' He kissed her hair, then looked into her eyes with a little flame burning steadily in his eyes. 'Are you really sure you want to take me on, Chattie Winslow?'

'Certain sure,' she responded. 'Will you?'

'Marry you? Just let anyone try and stop me—I'll be honoured to.'

Three and a half weeks later, six light planes were parked on the Mount Helena airstrip, a variety of four-wheel drive vehicles stood outside the garden gate and a ceremony was about to take place on the front lawn.

Before a table clothed in white linen with a gossamer silver over-cloth, the crowd gathered were all in their Sunday best with many a colourful hat, and many a suit that had come out of mothballs.

Merlene was wearing a skirt rather than jeans for the first time for years. Brett was full of importance in a proper little suit and in charge of Rich, who had silver wedding bells on his collar.

Joan Jackson was there looking elegant but slightly harassed. Jack Barlow was alongside Bill and the other station workers.

Steve Kinane stood in front of the table in a dark suit with his brother Mark beside him, acting as his best man, and fiddling with the very new gold wedding band on his left hand. And the marriage celebrant glanced expectantly at the main steps to the homestead.

Just then a hum went through the crowd as Harriet and Bridget emerged through the front door as a recording of the 'Wedding March' rang out.

They both looked lovely in off-the-shoulder gowns, Harriet's in jacaranda-blue, Bridget's in hyacinth-pink, and they carried white bouquets. As they began to descend the steps, another, louder hum rose as Chattie appeared on Slim's arm.

Without his trademark pony-tail, few people would

have recognized Slim in a well-tailored grey suit, blue shirt and navy tie.

But it was Chattie towards whom all eyes were drawn as she paused at the top of the steps. Her dress was stunning. Pure white heavy satin, it was a strapless sheath with a small train. Over it she wore a bolero of delicately flower-patterned voile with puff sleeves and a stand-up collar encrusted with seed pearls.

A froth of veil beneath a pearl coronet covered her loose hair and face; she wore short white gloves and carried white roses starred with single blue agapanthus florets.

As she paused, she wasn't conscious of the crowd of guests, however, she was looking back over the last few weeks and some of the surprises they'd contained.

Bridget, for example, had refused even to consider a double wedding on the grounds that Chattie's special day should be hers alone.

'We'll do our wedding our way,' she'd said.

Accordingly, a week earlier, they'd all flown to the Gold Coast, the Barlows and the Jacksons as well, and Mark and Bridget had been married in the chapel of the private school both Mark and Steve had attended, then enjoyed a lively reception at a restaurant overlooking the beach.

But the biggest surprise, perhaps, had been Steve's insistence that they continue to be 'traditional' until their wedding day.

Nestled in his arms when he'd made the declaration, Chattie had thanked him gravely but expressed the doubt that they could handle the strain. He'd then embarked on a discourse on the efficacy of cold showers—until she'd been helpless with laughter.

'If you think it's funny—' He looked at her re-proachfully.

'I do.'

'Well, I don't.' But he started to laugh too. Then he sobered. 'I suspect it will be good for my soul, a bit of discipline, but I also think, in your heart of hearts, you'd like to do it this way?' He searched her eyes.

'I must seem very old-fashioned but, yes, I would.'

'It's one of the things I love about you, Chattie. Your principles and your values.'

She came out of her reverie and walked down the steps on Slim's arm. There was, literally, not a cloud in the sky, and half an hour later as Steve raised her veil and kissed her the congregation cheered and Rich barked joyfully.

After the reception, Steve flew them to Brisbane where they picked up a commercial flight and winged their way to Cairns then drove north to Palm Cove.

They had the honeymoon suite in a marvellous hotel on the beach. Chattie looked round at the Javanese inspired décor of terracotta floor tiles, lovely fretted woodwork, bamboo and batik, the four poster-bed, and sighed with pleasure.

'There's more,' Steve said and took her hand to lead her out to their private courtyard with its own swim-ming pool and spa. He put his arms around her. 'Did I tell you what a stunning bride you made?'

She wrinkled her nose at him. 'Several times actu-ally. Did I tell you that you took my breath away in a suit?'

'Several times, actually. Here's one thing I haven't

told you—I'm dying by degrees. Have been for over a month, come to think of it.'

'So have I. May I suggest a solution?'

'Be my guest.'

'A swim and a spa to freshen us up.' She paused as he looked alarmed, but continued resolutely, 'A leisurely consumption of those gorgeous pink cocktails they provided, to relax us, then—anything is possible.'

'I'm so glad you got to that bit. I had a horrible feeling you were going to recommend we went out for dinner as well!'

She looked into his dark eyes then stood on her toes to cup his face. 'As a matter of fact, I'm quite happy to reverse the—order of things.'

'Like this?' He started to kiss her.

Five minutes later Chattie was trembling against him with every nerve of her body pulsing, or so it felt.

'Steve,' she whispered raggedly.

'Come,' he answered, and picked her up to set her down on her feet again next to the bed. And he began to undress her item by item, stopping every so often to caress her.

Her going away outfit was a short-sleeved aquamarine linen suit. He took the jacket off and drew an unsteady breath because her bra was also aquamarine trimmed with white. He smiled into her eyes, and she smiled, wryly, back.

Then he reached for the zip of her skirt, and as it slipped down her legs matching briefs were revealed, plus a lacy garter belt holding up pale stockings.

She stepped out of the skirt and he put his hands on her waist and raised his eyebrows at her. 'Twenty-one?'

'Yes. You were right, thirty-two, twenty-one, thirty-two.'

'And all of it gorgeous. Especially these.' His hands moved to her hips. 'They have a way of swishing that is—was,' he amended, 'a sore trial to me.'

Chattie moved beneath his hands and slipped her arms around his waist. 'So you told me.'

'At least you're not cross about it this time.' His lips twisted.

'No. The opposite,' she said ruefully. 'May I?' And, without waiting for an answer, started to unbutton his shirt.

From then on things got quite hectic as they undressed each other and gloried in each other's bodies.

'I was wrong,' he said with an effort at one stage. 'Nearly everything about you drives me insane. Your lovely, satiny skin, your breasts, your perfume.' He stopped talking and buried his head beneath her breasts.

Then he picked her up again and laid her on the bed and lay down beside her. And what he did to her breasts and nipples with his hands and teeth brought her almost more delight than she could bear.

'Please,' she said on a sobbing little breath as she arched her body and tangled her fingers in his hair.

He raised his mouth and kissed her on the lips until she quietened. Then he slid his leg between hers and started to stroke her thighs with his fingers moving ever higher to that secret place that was at the core of her delight. And only when he felt her grow wet with desire did he ease his weight onto her and smile down into her eyes.

'How am I doing?' he asked her softly.

'Steve, I…got the feeling this would be a soul-liberating experience…between us,' she said disjointedly, 'I was right. You're *wonderful* and—'

But she couldn't go on because a shudder racked him and he said no more. But everything he did to her and the way he did it drew a rapturous response from her, until that moment when she was completely exposed to him and he claimed her for his own.

And, as they'd climbed the pinnacle of ecstasy together, so they came down in each other's arms, breathing heavily, dewed with sweat and immensely moved.

'That was…' Chattie paused '…like nothing else that's ever happened to me.'

He stroked her hair off her face. 'I didn't hurt you?'

'No,' she said wonderingly. 'There was so much pleasure I didn't even stop to think about it.'

He held her hard. 'So much pleasure,' he repeated. 'I can't even begin to tell you how much pleasure you bring me, soul and body.'

She breathed contentedly.

'Although,' he added, 'I have to tell you that discipline in these matters has become a thing of the past, Miss Winslow-that-was.'

She laughed softly and traced the line of his jaw. 'I have to tell you that, for a teacher, I've developed a strange aversion to discipline.'

He caught her wandering fingers and kissed them. 'I'm extremely glad we agreed to come away immediately after the reception.'

'Oh? So am I, but—why?'

'They'll party on for days.'

Chattie eased herself up on her elbow and as the

sheet slipped pulled it up to cover her breasts. 'Days!' she said incredulously. 'Without us?'

'Yep.' He pulled the sheet down.

'That's…unusual, isn't it?' She automatically reached for the sheet again but his fingers stopped hers.

'Why so modest?' His dark eyes glinted.

She coloured delicately. 'Habit, maybe?'

He pulled her into his arms. 'I was going to suggest a shower, a swim in the nude in our pool, then a spa, sipping those cocktails. Think you could cope?'

She opened her mouth, closed it, then said, 'Not until you tell me whether you're joking about them partying on for days without us.'

'I'm not joking,' he said solemnly. 'Old outback custom. Do you mind?'

'No. It's not my place to, anyway. I just—'

'Oh, but it is now you're Mrs Steve Kinane,' he interrupted.

Chattie lay back. 'I hadn't thought of it like that. But I certainly wouldn't interfere with any old outback customs.'

'What about customs affecting newly-weds?'

'Popping around in the nude and the like, do you mean?' she queried with the utmost gravity.

'Uh-huh.'

'I will…' her lips started to curve '…do my best!'

He hugged her until she could barely breathe, then looked into her eyes. 'You do know that I'd be lonely to the depths of my soul without you now. I *love* you.'

CHAPTER ELEVEN

TWELVE months later to the day, Patrick Charles Kinane was born to Charlotte and Steve Kinane, on their wedding anniversary. He was named after his grandfathers. Two and a half years later his sister, Francesca Christine Kinane, arrived.

By this time, Rich not only had Brett and Patrick to play with, but Brett's twin brothers, Luke and Jonathan, born nine months after Harriet had left the station the day after Chattie had first arrived at Mount Helena. And, on their frequent visits, Mark and Bridget's daughter, Louella, joined in. Mark and Bridget remained blissfully in love and his career as a racehorse trainer was going well.

Both Slim and Merlene still worked at the homestead in amicable disharmony and Miss Daisy, retired from racing, had produced a filly foal.

It was at Francesca's—universally known as Bubbles—christening that Steve Kinane looked around the garden at the festivities, and festivities they were. Once more there were planes on the airstrip and vehicles at the garden gate. Once again many of the district wore their Sunday best and a veritable feast had been produced. This time, though, there was a growing tribe of children underfoot.

But he couldn't see the person he sought so he went in search of his wife.

He found her in their bedroom. She'd just put the

baby down and was buttoning up her blouse. He closed the door and watched her, saying nothing. In nearly four years Chattie Winslow, as he still sometimes thought of her, had changed little.

Still the same fair curly hair, the musical laugh, the person you could depend on. Her figure was fuller but still enchanting and she had the lovely bloom and radiance of a contented mother and wife.

If it was possible, he reflected, he was more in love with her than ever—and more content himself than he would have believed possible.

'Why so serious?' she asked lightly as she came towards him. 'Don't tell me, Luke and Patrick are fighting? Merlene and Slim have fallen out? There's been a power failure or there's a storm lurking? Harriet is giving someone a piece of her mind or—'

He put a finger on her lips. 'None of those, although on past history they're all entirely possible. No. I just wanted to be alone with you.'

'Why?' she asked seriously, although her eyes were dancing.

'I have some matters on my mind, really weighty ones.'

'Oh, dear! That sounds ominous.'

'Mmm,' he agreed and looked her up and down from beneath half-closed lids. 'Much as I like this blouse—' he put his fingers on a couple of buttons '—and I think your skirt is very elegant—I would also like to rip them off and have my way with you here and now.'

She closed her fingers over his. 'Much as I *love* the sound of that, Steve, we are in the middle of a christening party.'

He took her in his arms. 'I have a solution. How about we muster this mob off to their prospective homes? They've been here all day anyway.'

Chattie slid her arms around his neck and looked thoughtful. 'Well, in about an hour Patrick will be ready for an early supper and bed. Bubbles has had such a big day, I confidently expect her to sleep for hours.'

'All of which means?' He stroked some of her curls behind her ear.

'The moon should be full tonight, so, when it rises, we could have a moonlit champagne supper ourselves—and an early night.'

'Done,' he replied and kissed her. 'I'll go and speed up the mustering process.'

'Just don't be too...obvious about it.' She looked comically alarmed.

'Obvious? Me? Whatever gave you that idea?'

'You did!'

'Listen, can we take a roll-call of our sentiments on the subject?' he asked rapidly and almost in military style.

Chattie removed her arms from his neck and he released her.

'Is it or is it not a known fact that, with very little prompting, our friends can sometimes take days to be gotten rid of?'

'Old outback custom—it has been known,' she answered precisely.

'Would it be fair to say—' his dark eyes roamed over her in a way she knew well and one that always thrilled her '—that, historically, when things get to this stage between us there is only one way to handle it?'

She moistened her lips but said crisply, 'That would be an accurate interpretation.'

His gaze rested on the hollows at the base of her throat where a little pulse was beating wildly.

'Then, having done our duty to our maximum ability, are we united in a desire to rid Mount Helena of all extraneous persons with courtesy, naturally, but also speed?'

'So long as you take responsibility for overturning old outback customs—' Chattie clicked her heels and saluted 'we are! I'll come and help you.'

But she collapsed against him, laughing, and he kissed her thoroughly before they left the room, hand in hand.

The world's bestselling romance series.

HARLEQUIN®
Presents

Seduction and Passion Guaranteed!

THEPRINCESSBRIDES

For duty, for money...for passion!

Discover a thrilling new trilogy from a rising star of Harlequin Presents®, Jane Porter!

Meet the Royals...

Chantal, Nicolette and Joelle are members of the blue-blooded Ducasse family. Step inside their sophisticated and glamorous world and watch as these beautiful princesses find they have to marry three international playboys—for duty, for money... and definitely for passion!

Don't miss

THE SULTAN'S BOUGHT BRIDE (#2418)
September 2004

THE GREEK'S ROYAL MISTRESS (#2424)
October 2004

THE ITALIAN'S VIRGIN PRINCESS (#2430)
November 2004

Pick up a Harlequin Presents® novel and you will enter a world of spine-tingling passion and provocative, tantalizing romance!

Available wherever Harlequin books are sold.

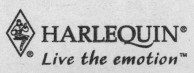

HARLEQUIN®
Live the emotion™

www.eHarlequin.com

like a phantom in the night comes
a new promotion from

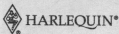 **HARLEQUIN®**

INTRIGUE®

GOTHIC ROMANCE

Beginning in August 2004, we offer you
a classic blend of chilling suspense and
electrifying romance, starting with....

A DANGEROUS INHERITANCE
LEONA KARR

And don't miss a spine-tingling Eclipse tale each month!

September 2004
MIDNIGHT ISLAND SANCTUARY
SUSAN PETERSON

October 2004
THE LEGACY OF CROFT CASTLE
JEAN BARRETT

November 2004
THE MAN FROM FALCON RIDGE
RITA HERRON

December 2004
EDEN'S SHADOW
JENNA RYAN

Available wherever Harlequin books are sold.
www.eHarlequin.com

HIECLIPSE

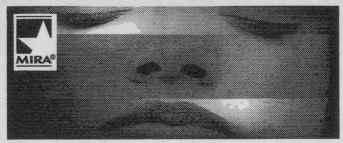

"Twisted villains, dangerous secrets…irresistible."
—*Booklist*

New York Times Bestselling Author

STELLA
CAMERON

Just weeks after inheriting Rosebank, a once-magnificent Louisiana plantation, David Patin was killed in a mysterious fire, leaving his daughter, Vivian, almost bankrupt. With few options remaining, Vivian decides to restore the family fortunes by turning Rosebank into a resort hotel.

Vivan's dream becomes a nightmare when she finds the family's lawyer dead on the sprawling grounds of the estate. Suddenly Vivian begins to wonder if her father's death was really an accident…and if the entire Patin family is marked for murder.

Rosebank is not in Sheriff Spike Devol's jurisdiction, but Vivian, fed up with the corrupt local police, asks him for unofficial help. The instant attraction between them leaves Spike reluctant to get involved—until another shocking murder occurs and it seems that Vivian will be the next victim.

kiss them goodbye

"Cameron returns to the wonderfully atmospheric Louisiana setting…for her latest sexy-gritty, compellingly readable tale of romantic suspense."—*Booklist*

*Available the first week of October 2004,
wherever paperbacks are sold!*